RAINDROPS ARE FALLING ON MY HEAD

Ajoy Mundkur

ISBN

Hardcase 979-8-89744-675-9
Paperback 979-8-89673-821-3

Miss you Mum

Contents

About the Author

Ajoy Mundkur has more than 3 decades of multi-sector Industry experience across Consumer Durables, Lubricants, Paints and Speciality Chemicals. A Senior business professional, he is also a Business Consultant and Director, Nexon Paints, Hyderabad

An MBA in Marketing from SIMSR, Mumbai, he has been featured in "25 Most Valuable CEO's of India" in 2021 by the Business Connect Magazine. He is voracious reader, fitness enthusiast and an avid cricket fan.

A passionate believer in the environment and sustainability, he has cofounded Green2Go Pvt.Ltd.- A company that recycles plastic waste into travel products. With this initiative he aims in his own small way, to contribute to a better world.

Raindrops are Falling on my Head, is his first book. Set within the fiction genre, each of these seven short stories have intriguing characters, and encapsulates their attempt to try and navigate through the issues that confront them.

You can connect with him on:

https://www.Facebook.com/Ajoy Mundkur
https://www.Linkedin.com/Ajoy Mundkur
https://www.Instagram.com/ajoymundkur

All proceeds from the sale of this book will go to Suryoday Trust, (https://suryodaytrust.org) an NGO that works with children with intellectual disability.

Acknowledgements

Writing a book, for a first-time author is a tough job. One's self-belief is continuously challenged. I always had this fondness to write, but never really took it seriously, nor had the time.....until Covid struck. Suddenly, all work at the office came to a standstill and I found myself with a lot of time on my hands.

Little did I know that what began as a satirical write up on the origins and fall out of the disease would receive positive feedback from friends and family, and would encourage and push me to write six more, resulting in this book!

A big thanks and shout out to my wife and son who motivated me to write. My friends and well-wishers who egged me on, and to Ms. Himali Kothari whose Creative Writing Workshop helped me in polishing my writing skills.

Déjà Vu

Session 1:

"Good evening, doctor," said Madhav Nair, who had just seated himself in the clinic of Dr. Raveendran, a renowned psychotherapist in Mumbai.

"Hello Madhav, how are you?" asked the doctor.

"I'm good doctor," said Madhav.

"Well, let's see what we have got here," the doctor continued. "Just confirming a few details before we start. In your personal history, you have mentioned that you are 46 years old, married with two kids, a boy whose name is Aakash, aged 15, and a girl, Samaira, who is 13. You're the only son of your parents, and both your parents are no more. Your wife's name is Namrata; she is a housewife. You're a Computer Engineer by education, you work with Syscom Teleservices in their Engineering Services Department. Is my understanding correct?"

"Yes, doctor, that's me in a nutshell."

"Good," said the doctor, and then added, "What brings you here, Madhav? What is the nature of your problem? How can I help you?"

"I really don't know how to explain this, doctor…"

"I'm a psychologist, Madhav. You can share your innermost thoughts with me, whatever you think is your problem, and we will both try to find a solution to it. A solution that will hopefully work for you. My role will be that of an enabler and facilitator. Finally, it is you who will have to find a solution to your problem. So shed all your inhibitions and talk to me as frankly as possible."

"Yes, doctor, and that's why I've made an appointment to see you, but my problem, if at all it is a problem, is so... so... difficult to explain that I'm not sure how I should describe it."

"Start from the very beginning," said the doctor. "When did you first notice it...this problem?"

"I may have been about 8 years old," said Madhav, his voice trailing off.

"8? What exactly happened, Madhav?"

"Our pet dog Gonzo died."

Years of training as a psychologist had taught him to always empathise with and draw the patient out. Make the patient pour out their innermost thoughts. The more he understood the patient's psychological makeup, the easier it was to prescribe a solution.

"Oh! It must have been quite a shock to you. I can imagine you must have really loved Gonzo. Pets become very close, even family, to many people. Getting over the loss of a pet can be as traumatic as losing a very close family member. Was it the grief of Gonzo's passing that affected you?"

"It was, indeed, doctor. I was an only child, so Gonzo was the only 'friend and playmate' I had at home. It was a huge blow and took me quite a while to come to terms with his passing, but that's not really what the problem is...."

Oh really! This is interesting.... in that case, what is it that you would define as your problem?"

"About a week before he died, I had a dream that Gonzo would die. And he died exactly the way I saw it in my dream. I had taken him out for a walk; when he saw another dog on the other side of the road. He jumped hard, freed himself from his leash, ran onto the road, chased after the other dog when a speeding car came out of nowhere and ran over him."

"Oh, that's really sad," said the doctor, in a tone that showed complete sympathy with what Madhav had just told him. "But such things can happen, they are not unheard of. It's possible that some fear in your subconscious mind manifested itself in a dream, and by sheer coincidence, it turned out to be reality. Rare, but not uncommon..."

"Doctor, from that day onwards, I've noticed that it happens quite regularly to me"

"Er, regularly...? By that you mean?"

"The second incident that I can recall, happened just after my 10th standard exam. I was about sixteen then. My parents and I were going on holiday after my exams. We had booked this resort in Chiplun called Riverview Lodge. Dad was driving the car. I was seated next to him; mum was seated in the rear. We left our home in Mumbai at about 7 am. At around 1 pm, we stopped for lunch. After a hearty lunch, we restarted. A full stomach and the fresh countryside breeze ensured that both mum and I soon dozed off. Seeing us sleeping, I guess dad momentarily dozed off as well. The next thing we know is that there is a loud noise, and when we open our eyes, we see the car has smashed into a tree. The impact caused the hood to buckle. This was a good 30 years ago. Cars didn't have airbags then. The steering wheel hit dad on the head, and he possibly died on the spot. Mum and I were in shock with some injuries but were not incapacitated. A group of people from the nearby village gathered, pulled out Dad, and took him to the nearest hospital, where he was declared dead."

The doctor took a good 10-15 seconds to process what he had just heard. "Good God!" he exclaimed, horrified at what he had just heard. Then after another pause, he continued, "Life can sometimes be very cruel. What a horrible experience at such a young and impressionable age for you. Kudos to you and your mum for coming out the right side of this horrendous incident. I can think of several others who would not have been able to cope with the magnitude of the tragedy."

"Mum was heartbroken and passed away some 4-5 years after dad's accident, but with supreme mental effort and willpower, I have somehow managed to put the whole incident behind me and move on."

"Well, that's commendable, well done, young man," said the doctor. "It is quite normal for you to be carrying some mental scars from an incident as devastating as this."

"But, that's not really my problem," said Madhav

Before the doctor could react, he added, "I had dreamt of this exactly a fortnight ago, even before my exams started."

"What? Really?"

"Yes, doctor, and I remember I mentioned it to both mum and dad when I had the dream. They said I was overly stressed due to the long hours of studying. Mum said dad was an expert driver who had been driving for 30 years in Mumbai without so much as a scratch on the car. Nothing like that will happen they said. It was only a dream, so I should relax."

After several seconds of silence, the doctor continued, "There appears to be a pattern to your dreams. Post a tragic incident in your life, you seem to believe that you had seen it in your dream sometime earlier. Could it be possible you think, that the incident happens, and then your mind somehow makes you believe that you had seen it earlier in a dream?"

"No doctor, you must believe me when I say this. The dreams I have, always predate the actual incidents. I can't prove them to you because both the events have already happened, but they do. I don't know how I can make you believe me, but please, trust me." said Madhav

"I trust you, Madhav, that's not what I'm trying to say. Sometimes, our brain and psyche play games with us and make us believe what we want to believe. I am not saying you are deliberately making this up. But the fact is that we humans do have a subconscious mind, which, as Sigmund Freud said, is very powerful and makes us sometimes believe things to be real even when they are not."

"I am not making this up, doctor," said Madhav, and then went completely silent

"I'm not saying that you are making it up." said the doctor. "Rather, what I'm saying is that your mind could be imagining things without you even knowing it. It can happen when people have had traumatic events in their life like you have." After a short pause, he continued. "Relax Madhav, it's just our first session. Over the last hour or so, we have had a very interesting chat. I must confess that what you have described is extremely rare but not unheard of. I do need to have some more discussion with you on this, so what we will do is fix up for another session next week; if that's okay with you."

"Yes, doctor, next week at the same time is fine."

"Great. And remember to use this week to write down all the dreams you have experienced and which later came true. I want to know each one of them, I want to understand these events better, and let me try and see how I can help you."

"The problem, doctor, is that due to these dreams, I'm afraid to go to sleep because I just don't know when I'll get one of these dreams, and now with this track record, I am so afraid that they could come true. It's scary, to say the least. For the past several years, I haven't known what it is to sleep well for a full 7-8 hours. I set up the alarm every 2 hours just so that

I don't get into the REM sleep stage, which is where, from what I've read, all the dreams occur."

"Has any medical doctor advised you of this? You will destroy yourself if you keep doing this night after night," said the doctor.

"No doctor has advised me on this. I read about REM sleep and when we get our dreams on the Internet."

"I tell you; this Internet and WhatsApp medicine will prove to be the biggest bane of medical science. Don't worry and get yourself a good night's sleep. That's possibly what you really need the most. Do you have difficulty getting to sleep?"

"Yes, doctor, I find it difficult to get any meaningful sleep with this routine. I'm always tired and can't do my best at work. I've been getting average ratings in all my annual appraisals. My peers have got promotions and are in more senior positions compared to where I am in the organisation. My family and friends tell me I'm always irritated and have these horrible mood swings."

"I think it's all because you haven't been sleeping well. I'll prescribe you some medication. Take this tablet once at night after dinner, and you will sleep well, trust me," said the doctor, who then proceeded to write out a prescription on his letter pad, which he handed over to Madhav.

"Thank you so much, doctor. We'll meet again next week, same time."

"Yup," said the doctor, "See you next week and let me know how your sleeping went. If you sleep well, you will do well."

"Goodbye, doctor," said Madhav and left the clinic.

Session 2:

"Good evening, doctor." said Madhav

"Good evening, Madhav, how are you doing? How was the past week?"

"Nothing eventful," said Madhav. "I took the tablets that you prescribed, have been sleeping like a log at night. Haven't had any dreams as such, so I feel great, and what's more, even my colleagues in the office remarked that I was looking far more energetic than they have seen me in the past."

"That is so wonderful to hear," said the doctor. "I'm so happy to hear that you're doing well already!"

"I've made a list of all the major dreams that I have had, doctor," said Madhav. "Just like you asked me to."

"Okay," said the doctor. "Let's see what they look like. Please continue."

"In our last session, you said that it was only the bad things that I dreamt of. But that's not true. There have been some 'good' dreams as well which have also come true," said Madhav.

"Tell me about them," said the doctor.

"This one was about getting admission into JK College of Engineering," said Madhav. "My PCM (Physics,

Chemistry, Maths) marks in the 12ᵗʰ standard were 92%, which was below the cutoff required to get admission into JK, which was around 98% at the time. I had got admission into the slightly lower-ranked TS College of Engineering, but my heart was not in it. JK was the best Engineering college in the city where I wanted to study and graduate from."

"And then what happened?" asked the doctor, "Did you manage to get into JK?"

"Yes, I did," said Madhav, "A good month after the 1ˢᵗ semester had started. You see, I was on the waitlist at JK. May have been waitlist no. 20 or so. Anyway, it shouldn't have mattered because, once college and classes start, the waitlist is scrapped. In this case, the students as per the college's merit list had been admitted. They had already joined the college, and the semester had already begun."

"I'm really curious now," said the doctor. "How did you still manage to get into JK?"

"About a week before, I had a dream in which, well, I can't remember very clearly because it's been more than 20 years now, but from what I can recall, I was driving a car on the highway, when the vehicle before me, I think it was a van, met with an accident. I saw it tumble off the highway and into a ravine. I stopped my car. Peered into the ravine. I saw an explosion. There was no other car or person in sight on the highway - it was completely deserted. I was frightened. I took a U-turn and drove back home."

"How is the accident in your dream connected with your getting admission into JK?" asked the doctor

"A week later, the news was splashed all over the media about a bus carrying 30 students of first-semester engineering students of JK College meeting with an accident in the Bhor ghat. They were going to Satara for an Inter-Collegiate Engineering Quiz. It had been raining heavily, the driver lost control of the vehicle, and it plunged into a ravine about 100 metres deep. The fuel tank caught fire, and the vehicle exploded. No one survived the tragedy. About a week later, I received a call from the college saying that the first 30 waitlisted students were being contacted in case they were interested in joining."

"What?" exclaimed the doctor. "That's insane."

"Now you know how I feel, doctor," said Madhav, quietly feeling vindicated.

"If what you say is true," said the doctor, "there seems to be a clear pattern that I can identify. There is an accident or tragedy that happens in your life, and then depending on the context, it either helps you or it's a major blow for you. But there is always an accident or a tragedy that is involved. We need to investigate this further. My view is, it could be due to the passing away of your father in that gruesome accident, which has stayed with you in your subconscious mind. In short, it is stored away somewhere in the deep recesses of your mind. It keeps surfacing from time to time in the form of these accidents that you see in your dreams."

"Do you really think so?" Madhav asked.

"Could be, in fact, if you ask me, it's very much possible," said the doctor.

After a brief silence, Madhav continued, "Like this one other time, there was a Project Engineer requirement for a 6-month international assignment in Switzerland. Those interested had to apply for the position on our internal company portal. A committee comprising senior managers of the company, was appointed to scrutinise the applications. This was something I wanted very badly. Switzerland of all places, my dream destination, and getting to spend 6 months there! I was sure that I would bag it. However, despite having all the right credentials, the committee chose Senthil, another engineer and a colleague of mine, who they felt was more suitable for the project. I was very disappointed. I went home that evening, had a few drinks to drown my sorrow, and crashed out."

"And then what happened?" asked the doctor

"That night I had a dream," continued Madhav as the doctor listened attentively, wondering what it is that Madhav will have to say. "In my dream that night, I was alone, walking on the street, standing below a building when I happened to look up. On the 5th floor of the building, I see a girl, maybe around 10 years old, just jump off the balcony. She falls to the ground, lying there in a pool of blood. I could clearly see… there was lots of crying and weeping. An ambulance appears, she is rushed to the hospital, her parents accompany her."

Silence prevailed in the room. Then, after a few moments, Madhav continued.

"The dream made no sense to me. What the bloody hell is this?" I asked myself before I got out of bed. "Maybe it's because of the hangover from the drinks I had last evening, the disappointment of not making it to Switzerland," I told myself.

"Meanwhile, Senthil got his visa done and was due to go to Switzerland in about a week when his daughter fell seriously ill. She was diagnosed with Meningitis and had to be hospitalised. She was serious enough to be in the ICU. The doctors said it was touch and go with her chances, as the fever was raging at 104°F plus, and just wouldn't come down despite all their efforts and medication. The poor chap, Senthil had to cancel his trip to be with his daughter. My company nominated me to go as Senthil's replacement, and that's how I eventually did make the trip."

"And what happened to Senthil's daughter?" the doctor asked.

"Oh! She survived. Her condition gradually improved and in a couple of weeks, she was discharged. She is good friends with my kids; they are of the same age group, they hang out quite a bit," said Madhav, much to the doctor's relief.

"Well, I must admit, that you have a unique problem here. I researched your problem during this last week," said the doctor. "From what you describe and our discussions thus far, I can say that there is a medical term for your condition

- Oneirophrenia. It is a hallucinatory dream-like state in patients. The severity of this condition can range from derealisation to complete hallucination and delusions."

"So, you think that I'm a nutjob, that I'm delusional?" said Madhav, now clearly angry and irritated.

"Relax, Madhav. As a doctor, I am just doing a clinical diagnosis based on what I have heard and understood from you," said the doctor, his voice calm but firm. He had dealt in the past with such patients who refused to accept his diagnosis. It was quite normal to encounter such type of patients in his field of work.

"So, you think I just imagine all of this; despite telling you of all the instances of the post-dream event happening exactly as I dreamt of it," said Madhav, outraged at the doctor's diagnosis of him as having a mental issue.

Realising that Madhav was agitated, the doctor tried to reason with him, by appealing to his logical and rational mind. "If you recall Madhav, during all our conversations and discussions, you have provided **NO EVIDENCE** to prove the event is a post-dream occurrence. There is no video with a time and date stamp of pre-dream and post-dream. There is not even a diary or a journal that you have maintained, where you could have written down the sequence of events pre and post. You describe the event and then you say that I dreamt of it. Think of it, Madhav, there is no scientific explanation to explain that what you see in a dream can manifest itself. There could be the occasional coincidence, but can it happen time after time? It just can't be possible, right? You're a qualified, educated person, just think about it, does it make sense to you?"

"Fine doctor. If that's what you think, I have nothing more to say," said Madhav. He got up from the chair he was seated on.

"Wait," said the doctor. "Don't lose your temper, Madhav. As I said, I was only trying to arrive at a clinical diagnosis of what I think is your problem. There is no need for you to be agitated or angry at me. I'm just doing my job, for which you sought my help."

Madhav began to leave for the door when the doctor said, "Let's try one more time, Madhav. You said that you have been sleeping well now with the medications that I prescribed during our consultation. Is that right?" asked the doctor.

"Yes," said Madhav.

"Okay, good. The next time you have a dream, please write it in a notebook or record it on a video or something and then see me immediately. We will make a note of it. Then we wait for one week, two weeks, three weeks, whatever time it takes between the dream and reality and see whether it really happens or not. If it does, I, despite being a man of science, will believe you. I will put my hands up and say this is a supernatural power you have been bestowed with, which medical science has no answer to." He then whipped out his cell phone and asked Madhav, "Tell me your number, Madhav."

Madhav gave him his number.

He dialled the number, Madhav's phone rang. He then disconnected the call. "This is my personal number," he said. "Please save it, and I will save your number as well," he continued. "Don't call my secretary. Call me directly. I will take your call however busy I happen to be, and we meet up that very day. Let's prove this 'Dreams come true hypothesis' as either true or false with evidence and data. Is that okay with you?"

"Okay doctor," said Madhav. "I will get back to you as soon as I get my next dream.

Thanks, doctor, goodbye," he said and left the room.

Session 3:

Madhav woke up with a start, his entire body covered in a cold sweat. For about a month after the last session with the doctor, he had experienced no dreams as such. He was sleeping well, and was beginning to believe that all he had experienced was indeed some kind of a chimera, an illusion, with no connection to reality. He even was beginning to come to terms with the fact that maybe the doctor was right after all. Maybe he did imagine that he dreamt of it after the event.

But last night he did get the dreaded dream, and what he saw last night shook him up to his very core. As the doctor had instructed, he clicked on the camera icon of his phone, then clicked on the record button, and started to record his dream in as detailed a manner as he possibly could. He then proceeded to call the doctor as he was instructed, but there was no response. So, he sent a few WhatsApp messages and waited for the doctor's reply.

∞

Dr Raveendran was in a counselling session with one of his patients when his cell phone rang. As a matter of professional etiquette, and since he didn't want to be distracted when he was in a counselling or therapy session with a patient, he would put his phone on silent and hand it over to his secretary. After he was done with the patient, his secretary would hand him back the phone, and he would check to see if any call or message needed his attention.

When his secretary handed him his phone post a session with a patient, the doctor saw that there were 2 missed calls and 3 WhatsApp messages from Madhav.

Message 1: Hello doctor, good evening, this is Madhav.

Message 2: You had asked me to call you when I had my next dream. I had a dream last night. I tried calling you twice to inform you, but you didn't pick up my call.

Message 3: Please return my call when you are free. Consider it urgent, please. Thanks.

"Two missed calls and three messages from Madhav. Isn't he the patient with whom you have had two sessions?" she asked

"Yes," said the doctor. "I had asked him to call me when he had his next dream."

He looked at his watch. There were still 15 minutes before the next appointment. He asked his secretary to make him a cup of tea. Then he called Madhav

A couple of rings before Madhav picked up.

"Hello Madhav, how are you?" asked the doctor.

"I am doing well, doctor," said Madhav.

"So finally, you did have your dream. What is it about a month since we last met?"

"Yes, doctor," said Madhav.

"Is it an accident again?" asked the doctor, sounding more sarcastic than concerned.

"Yes doctor."

"Told you." said the doctor. "Every dream of yours involves an accident. It's the mental scarring of your father's accident that keeps popping up. We may need to try hypnotic therapy to see if that can help. There were some studies conducted at Harvard on this with very good results." Then, as an afterthought, he added, "Who is the unfortunate soul this time around?"

There was complete silence at the other end.

"Hello Madhav, are you there?" asked the doctor. "Can you hear me?"

"Yes, doctor, I can hear you." said Madhav

"I was asking, who is the person in your dream this time?"

"Er… Doctor, it's best if I met you in person and spoke to you about this"

"OK, come over to my clinic this evening at 6 pm," said the doctor.

"OK doctor, this evening is fine. I'll see you at 6 at your clinic," said Madhav, and they both hung up.

ᔆ

Madhav reached Dr Raveendran's clinic 15 minutes before 6pm.

Just a little before 6 pm, the doctor reached his clinic and found Madhav waiting outside. He opened the door with his set of keys and ushered Madhav in.

Madhav rather nervously entered the doctor's cabin and sat down on the chair opposite the doctor. He appeared nervous and was clearly looking out of sorts.

"You're looking pale and ashen, Madhav. What's up? Here, have some water," said the doctor and then proceeded to offer Madhav a bottle of water from the refrigerator in his room.

Madhav took 3-4 long gulps and felt a bit better. He appeared more composed. Seeing this, the doctor said, "So, let's begin, Madhav. Tell me what you saw in your dream last night. Have you made a video recording of it like I had asked you to?"

"Yes, doctor, I did," said Madhav.

"Good," said the doctor. "Is it on your cell phone?"

"Yes," said Madhav,

"OK, let's push play and see what you have to say," said the doctor.

Madhav pulled out his cell phone, placed it on the table, navigated to video recordings and pressed play.

The video started to play. A pale-faced Madhav appeared on the screen. "Hello Doctor, I am recording this video as per your instructions. I am sure you will be shocked by what I have to say, as indeed I was and still am…"

"Last night, I dreamt about you, doctor."

"Wait, wait, wait, press pause, please," said the doctor.

Madhav pressed the pause button.

"You dreamt about me?" The doctor was visibly shocked.

"Yes doctor"

"Wow!" said the doctor. Then, after a reflective pause of a couple of moments, he said, "Okay, please continue."

Madhav pressed the pause button again, and the video restarted. "In my dream last night, I saw that you had gone out for your morning walk on the Carter Road promenade. It was early in the morning, say around 6-6.30. I stay far away from Bandra, but for some strange reason, I found myself there, but at a distance. I could see you, but you couldn't see me. You finished your walk and were walking home when a truck went over a speed breaker at speed. Next, I saw something from the truck fly out, and that metal object crashed into your head, and you collapsed. Then I saw people rushing around, running towards you trying to help. Someone called the ambulance. In some time, an ambulance arrived. You were lying motionless on the road. The people from the ambulance and a few other people lifted you and placed you inside the ambulance. The ambulance raced away, its lights and sirens blaring. It took you to the nearby Holy Family Hospital."

"What happened next?" asked the doctor.

"Somehow, I found myself at the hospital too. You were swiftly moved from the ambulance to casualty, where the doctors examined you and pronounced you dead. It is here that my dream ended, and I woke up."

For a couple of moments, there was complete silence. Then Madhav continued, "I am really worried about you doctor. If you do go for a morning walk, please do not do so for the next few weeks. This is my humble request to you. If anything were to happen to you, I will not be able to forgive myself. Doctor. I'm requesting you, please listen to me. Don't dismiss it as just another dream. In fact, I would say, stay put at home for the next few weeks."

"Oh, my goodness!" said the doctor. "Another accident, and this time it involves me! ME of all people!" And then he let out a loud roar of laughter and amidst guffaws said, "Madhav, the kind of things you come up with are simply insane!"

"Doctor, please listen to me for once and do not go for your morning walk for the next couple of weeks. I beg of you," said Madhav, his voice trembling, tears streaming down his eyes.

"Quite to the contrary, Madhav," said the doctor, "Yes, I do go for a morning walk to the Carter Road promenade. But rather than be scared and stay at home because of your dream, I would use it to prove to you that no such thing exists. That it's all in your mind. This is the first time that you have kept a record of your dream. What better opportunity for me as your doctor to go ahead and smash this 'dreams turn to reality theory' once and for all! This, I reckon, will be the best way to prove to you and possibly cure you of this monster that you are carrying in your head"

"Doctor, please listen to me..." Madhav pleaded

"No Madhav, now you listen to me. I will go for my morning walk as per my normal practice and here's what I will do. Every day when I finish my walk and reach home, I will send you a 'thumbs up' emoji. From what you've told me, your dreams come true within about 15 days, right? So, on the 16th day from today, when I WhatsApp you that thumbs up emoji, you must come over to my clinic and then we agree that the whole thing was a hoax, and you move on and begin your new life. Do we have a deal here?"

"Doctor, please listen…."

"Do we or do we not, Madhav? If you say no, I will be forced to believe that this is a charade that you are putting up. That you just wanted me to hear out your fanciful stories with no intention of resolving it. There can be no better opportunity to prove this one way or the other."

"I know you don't believe me, doctor, you think I'm delusional, but what if there is even that 1% chance that my dream does come true? Why do you want to risk your life?" asked Madhav.

"On a philosophical note, Madhav, our death is not always within our control. We can die at anytime, anywhere. That's just how uncertain life is, but for you to say that I have dreamt of it, and it will happen within 15 days, that's the kind of unscientific nonsense that I would like to smash to bits. And in doing so, if I can put sense into you and if that helps you lead a normal life, there could be no better job satisfaction. What's more, I can present your case as a case study at the World Convention of Psychotherapists in Scotland which is due later this year."

Silence prevailed in the room. Breaking the silence, the doctor asked, "So do we have a deal or not, Madhav?"

Madhav contemplated for a moment and then, with an air of resignation, said, "Okay, doctor, I will agree to everything that you said. But if things go as per my dream, don't blame me."

"If things go as per your dream, no one will be there to blame you, Madhav. Besides, I don't have any family, so no one will miss me. I live alone." Then he added, "Today is June 10th.

Note down the date for our next meeting in the clinic; it's June 26th at 7pm."

"I'll be there, doctor. Goodbye and good luck," said Madhav, and he left the clinic.

25th June:

It had been a tense 14 days for Madhav. Today was day fifteen. If nothing happened today, the monkey would be off his back. He could go back to living his life like normal people do. "God, please let today's day pass without any harm," Madhav prayed in his mind.

True to his word, over the past 14 days, the doctor kept sending the thumbs up emoji to Madhav between 7.30 and 8am, after the doctor got home from his morning walk. Madhav was beginning to believe that maybe the doctor was right, maybe he had imagined it all. That morning, Madhav finished his breakfast and was getting ready to go to the office. He glanced at his watch. It was 8 am. He looked at his cell phone. No thumbs up emoji from the doctor yet. A gnawing feeling in the pit of his stomach engulfed him. He was lost in thought… It can't happen again, surely not. Maybe the doctor had forgotten to WhatsApp after being so meticulous for the past 14 days. Maybe he is busy with something. I'll call him later in the day to inquire, he told himself.

∞

Jessica Gomindes, secretary to Dr. Raveendran, had been working with him for the past 5 years. Efficient, punctual, and very professional would be an apt description of what she brought to the table. She reached the clinic at her usual time of 9:30 am. The doctor would invariably be there by 9:45 am. The first appointment was usually at 10 am. The doctor's normal schedule was that he consulted patients from 10 am - 1 pm, and then in the evening from 7-9 pm. Since the doctor was always on time, she was a bit surprised when he did not turn up at the clinic even by 10 am. Maybe there was an unscheduled appointment, she thought. After waiting a while and when it was well past 10 am, she decided to call him.

"Hello," she said.

"Hello," an unknown voice picked up at the other end.

"Is this Doctor Raveendran on the line?" asked Jessica, surprised to note that someone else had answered the phone.

"This is Inspector Suryavanshi speaking from Bandra police station," said the voice at the other end.

"Oh, sorry, maybe I've dialed the wrong number," said Jessica.

"No Madam, you have dialled the right number. This is Doctor Raveendran's phone."

"Is he at the police station for some work? Is everything OK with him?" she asked.

"How are you related to the doctor?" the Inspector asked.

"My name is Jessica. I am his secretary."

"That's good. We were trying to go through the contact list on his phone to call a relative, but we couldn't access it as his phone was password-locked. Then, after a pause, he added, "Madam, I'm sorry, but I have to give you some really bad news."

"What is it, Inspector?" asked Jessica, still not able to comprehend what was going on.

"Dr. Raveendran died this morning in an accident."

"What?? I hope this is not some sort of a cruel prank that you are playing, mister. If it is, you had better watch out. The CM is a good friend of the doctor. I will ensure that you pay for this sick joke"

"No Madam, what I'm saying is true. This happened at about 7 am. He was returning home after his morning walk. He had reached the junction of Carter Road and Perry Road when a solid rectangle-shaped iron block fell off a truck and hit his head. Our police patrol van and an ambulance reached the spot within 5 minutes, but by the time we took him to Holy Family hospital, he was declared dead."

Jessica didn't know what to say. Stunned into silence, she was still unconvinced and believed this to be a prank.

"Extreme bad luck, Madam," the Inspector continued. The metal was being taken to a coastal road construction site. The truck had already passed the doctor when he was crossing the road. It went over a speed breaker at some speed, and the metal piece flew out. Unfortunately, the doctor was just behind the truck when the metal piece flew out, and hit him on the head.

"Is this for real? I still cannot believe what you're saying. How do I know that what you're saying is true?" Jessica asked.

"Yes, Madam, it's true. I am a policeman, why would I lie to you? Is the doctor married? Any wife, children, or anyone from his family whom we can inform?"

"No," said Jessica, "he lived alone. His parents passed away about 10 years ago, and he never got married. He would surely have some relatives, but I am not aware of anyone as such."

"Who is this Madhav who has called his number 3 times since the morning? When he hears my voice on the phone, he disconnects. When I try calling him from my phone, he doesn't pick up."

"Madhav?" said Jessica. "He is a patient of the doctor. The doctor has had two sessions with him. He is scheduled for a third one tomorrow."

"Maybe as his patient, he needs to speak to the doctor on some matter urgently," said the Inspector. "Can you inform him as well? Also, request you to come to the Bandra police station for some routine paperwork that needs to be done before we hand over the body. You can meet me once you're here. I will explain everything."

"I still can't believe this," Jessica could barely mumble.

"Such is life, madam. What will happen tomorrow, no one knows," said Inspector Suryavanshi, who paused briefly and disconnected.

26th June:

Madhav, as per his daily routine, read the newspaper along with his breakfast. His mind wandered to the calls he had made to the doctor yesterday. "Why is someone else picking up the call every time I call the doctor?" Madhav wondered. He had called the doctor three times yesterday morning, but someone else kept answering the call. He did receive a few calls from an unknown number but as was his wont, he never picked up calls from an unknown number. During the day, he was busy with his office work. With mid-year target deadlines just a few days away, there was no time at all for him to think of anything else. Browsing through the newspaper, on page 5, his attention went to the photograph of Dr. Raveendran in the obituary column.

With profound grief and sorrow, we, the Psychologists Association of India, inform of the untimely death of one of our finest and renowned psychologists, Dr. Raveendran, in an accident on the 25th of June 2022. There will be a prayer meeting for the departed soul at Chhabildas Centre, Turner Road, Bandra West from 4-6 pm.

"No, no, no, no. This can't be true," he told himself. In a stupor, he gulped down his tea, picked up the keys to his car, and dashed out of his home. "Where are you going in such a hurry? You haven't even changed from your home clothes. Finish your breakfast at least" his wife pleaded, startled at seeing him leave the house so abruptly.

He sat in his car and started it. He was in a daze. His mind was completely blank. He drove aimlessly. At the Vikhroli highway signal, he didn't see the red light, which he crossed. An oncoming truck had gathered pace and was coming towards his car at full speed. By the time the truck driver saw his car, it was too late….

It Must Have Been Love...

Vikram was engrossed in his laptop. Poring over spreadsheets, he was trying to make sense of the rows and columns of numbers.

A couple of days ago, his boss Sunil had called him into his room and fired him. "What's up with the sales numbers, Vikram? The kind of numbers you and your team are clocking doesn't even pay for your salary and travel. Get your act together or else things could get really bad for all of us. I've just gotten off the phone with the guys in Illinois, and let me tell you, they are very unhappy with how we are performing."

"How does one compete with the Chinese who sell their products at half of our price? Their government subsidizes manufacturing. This is an unequal fight," he had mumbled to himself.

He didn't notice his cabin door was open.

"Hello, Sir. I am Rajeshwari Reddy from the HR department. I have just joined today."

Vikram was caught by surprise. He looked up, his gaze met hers, and he just couldn't take his eyes off her. It's not that he hadn't seen good-looking women before, but she just took his breath away. She was beautiful in every sense of the word;

her face was flawless, with kohl-lined eyes, a slender nose, long tresses tied into a bun, dangling earrings, six bangles on each hand color-coordinated with the beige Kurti she had worn, and her full lips accentuated with fuchsia-colored lipstick. Her smile was like a million-watt lightbulb... He was gob smacked.

After a good 10 seconds of complete silence, she again repeated, "Hello, Sir."

Broken out of his trance, a very feeble "Hello" was all that he could muster. "Please have a seat."

"Thank you, sir," she said. Having pulled up a chair and seated herself, she continued, "Sir, I have been assigned the task of compiling the personal records of all employees. Some of the personal details pertaining to you are incomplete in our database, so I just wanted to check when I can meet you to get the details?"

"Day after tomorrow is good," he said, and then, looking into his calendar, he said, "It's a Friday, so that would be perfect, really. 10 am Friday."

"OK, Sir, I'll see you on Friday at 10. Thank you, sir," she said, then got up from the chair and walked towards the door. She opened the door and smiled back at him as she exited the room, shutting the door behind her.

He watched her leave. Her hip-swaying walk left him mesmerized. He stared at the door for a few seconds until she disappeared completely from his sight. He stared blankly at the wall to his right for a good minute or so and then finally, snapping out of his stupor, went back to his laptop.

A couple of hours later, his intercom buzzed, "Lunch?" It was Ganesh, the head of Finance. Vikram and Ganesh bonded well and invariably had lunch together. Two tables away, Debu, the head of HR, was seated with his HR team. The new joinee Rajeshwari, was there too. Their eyes met briefly, a brief smile flickered across both their faces, and then they looked away.

Did the new joinee from HR meet you? Ganesh was talking to Vikram over spoonsful of his favorite curd rice. "Yes, she met me. I've told her to meet me on Friday. Debu is young, straight out of XLRI and has a lot of new ideas. We need to support him. Let's see what changes he brings about in our company's HR," said Vikram as they concluded their lunch.

Thursday was his presentation to Sunil. It lasted all of two hours. Vikram was on the defensive, courtesy poor sales numbers in the first half of the year. His presentation focused on the new marketing campaign which was to be aired during the festive season, which he said would have a cascading effect on demand and would help differentiate the Teo Toys brand from the low-priced Chinese products. Through some cost-cutting measures which he had initiated, profit targets would be met even if sales were slightly below target.

Vikram was glad when the meeting with Sunil was over. He was looking forward to meeting Rajeshwari. Ever since he had seen her, there was a strange ache in his heart which he just couldn't fathom. He was very much married. Janaki, his wife, and he had first met at B School, fallen in love and five years later, got married. They had a six-year-old daughter, Kamini. As can sometimes happen with two highly qualified and career-minded working professionals, who are busy with their careers, their marriage had lost its spark. They were more like two individuals living under one roof, financially well-to-do, socially in the right place, but on a romantic level, there was no connection. Sex was rare, and rarer still was any love or affection that they felt or showed to each other.

"Good morning, Sir," Rajeshwari was in Vikram's room at 10 am sharp on Friday morning.

"Good morning, Rajeshwari."

Friday was Casual Day. She was in a turquoise blue t-shirt paired with a pair of jeans, a ponytail, lipstick, earrings, and no bangles.

"OK, tell me, what information does HR want from me?"

"Sir…"

"Can you please call me Vikram - that's the culture in our company. We all call each other by first names; designations don't really matter here."

"Ok, Sir. I mean Vikram, sir."

"Vikram," he said.

"Vikram," she repeated.

"Good. Shoot" he said

"We need to know your wife's name, her date of birth, your marriage anniversary date, how many children you have, their names, and dates of birth, and which school and class they go to." Then after a brief pause, she added, "And also your parents' names, contact numbers, and dates of birth."

"Wow! And why do you need all this information?"

"Debu Sir wants to send greetings from the company to the immediate families of each employee and organize special events on employees' anniversaries and their children's birthdays. He says we need to be like one big Teo Toys family and that's how the organization's productivity will improve."

"Ok, please note down. My wife's name is Janaki. She was born on 18 April 1965. We got married on 24 June 1993. We have one daughter, Kamini. She was born on 10 September 1999."

"Your parent…"

"Ah yes, my dad's name is Ashok. His date of birth is 15th April 1937. My mum's name is Shivangi. Her birthdate is 8th November 1940. They stay in Indiranagar. Their residence landline number is 080-25789653. Is there anything else you need to know?"

"No," she said. "Thank you very much, this should do nicely."

"Ok, bye,"

"I'll see you in the evening at the party," she added while getting up from her chair.

"Party…ah yes…. the party."

Vikram had forgotten about the party. As part of employee bonding, HR held a party for all the employees who had birthdays during the week. Since Teo Toys had 50-odd employees, practically every Friday evening was a party day. Debu had pushed Sunil to make attendance compulsory, especially for managers—he felt it would add to team bonding if managers were present. So, if you weren't travelling, then you had better attend.

"Yeah, I'll see you there," he said.

"Bye," she said, and exited the room, shutting the door behind her.

∾

Moheena Bhattacharya from Finance and Shreyas Jagtap from Sales had birthdays during the week. The Cyclone - a pub on Brigade Road, just a stone's throw from the Teo Toys office, was the default place for these parties. Trendy and hip, it was a youngsters' watering hole. A DJ, lots of dancing, with team and individual games; all contributing to making it a fun and happening event, especially for the youngsters.

At about 11:45 pm, as Vikram was winding up and getting ready to go, he found Debu approaching him.

"Vikram, can you do me a small favor?"

"Sure, chief. Tell me." said Vikram

"There is this new joinee, Rajeshwari, who stays in HSR layout, which is on the way to your house in Koramangala. There is no one else going that way. Since it's on the way for you, could you drop her, please?"

"Sure, no problem." said Vikram

Debu then gestured towards her. She joined them.

"Vikram will drop you home," Debu told her.

It was close to midnight; roads were deserted. The 6km journey from office to home which took all of 45 minutes in the morning traffic, would take only about 10 minutes. For the first 5 minutes, there was no conversation between them, then Vikram broke the ice, "So now that you know everything about me and my family, why don't you tell me something about yourself and your family?"

After an awkward pause, and somewhat hesitantly, Rajeshwari spoke up.

"My husband works in Dubai. I have a daughter who is 6 years old. Her name is Tamanaah."

"So you are in a long-distance marriage; must be quite tough," said Vikram

"My husband visits once a year, and we speak regularly over the phone."

"Yeah, but it must be quite tough on him. I have a six-year-old daughter as well. If I don't get to see her for one day or if I come home late and she has already gone to sleep, I feel terrible. Imagine him seeing her once a year. I'm sure he misses you'll a lot," said Vikram

"I would rather not talk about this," she said and stiffened up, clearly upset.

"Sorry, I didn't mean to upset you," Vikram was kicking himself for intruding into her personal space.

For the next five minutes, there was complete silence in the car.

"You can stop here," she said. "I live nearby."

He steered the car to the left and parked. She opened the door and got out of the car.

"Thanks for the lift. I really appreciate your help," she said.

"Sure, no problem," said Vikram.

"Bye, good night"

"Bye"

'Really stupid of me,' he told himself once she had left the car. In the next 5 minutes, he reached home.

His wife and daughter were fast asleep. He silently changed into his nightclothes and crashed into bed.

The entire next week passed by uneventfully. Come Friday, it was another birthday, another party. Close to midnight, as he prepared to leave she approached him directly and asked, "Vikram, can you please drop me like you did last time?"

"Sure, meet me on the porch."

After the previous experience, Vikram was chastened and hence he was silent. After five odd minutes of silence, which seemed like a lifetime, this time, she broke the ice.

"I lied to you last time. I'm sorry."

"Er…sorry, lied about what?" a surprised Vikram asked.

"That I'm married and my husband lives in Dubai."

OK….and?

"Well actually, I'm a divorcee; my husband and I separated about 5 years ago. Tamannah was about a year old. She wouldn't have any memory of him."

"Oh, I'm sorry to hear that. I didn't know…" Vikram sounded extremely apologetic.

"It's okay," she said. "It's not your fault, you didn't know. I live with my daughter and my mother. This job means everything to me. It gives me financial independence; it allows me and my family a fighting chance of surviving in this world."

"Yeah, for sure, and more power to you. I'm sure you will do very well with Teo Toys. Debu is a great guy to work with. Just keep working hard, and there is no reason why you shouldn't have a great career with us." Vikram was very happy that she hadn't taken last Friday's attempt at having a casual conversation with her negatively.

The junction where she had asked to be dropped off came up. He maneuvered the car to the left and parked.

"That's where you get off, I guess."

"Thanks a lot, Vikram, for the drop, but what I've told you is very confidential. No one in the company knows this."

"I will certainly not share it with anyone, you can rest assured. In fact, since I drive past this place to work every morning, why don't I pick you up from here, if that's okay with you? I pass by here by around 9"

"That will be nice. It will save me 30 minutes of my morning time. I normally board the company bus at 8:30"

"Ok great, see you on Monday morning at 9. Same place, other side of the road," he said and drove off after saying goodnight.

Come Monday morning, and Vikram saw her at the bus stop. She hopped in.

"Good morning, did you find the place easily?" he asked

"Yes, no problem."

"We can do this about 3-4 times a week, but when I travel, you're on your own," said Vikram.

"Yeah, that'll be fine," she said.

"I can even drop you home as well. I typically leave the office by 6-6:30."

"Oh, that will be nice. I can leave home late and reach home early."

"I too will have some company on an otherwise boring drive to and from the office"

At 9:30 am sharp, they reached the office. They got into the lift together; she exited at the 2nd floor where the HR department was based, and he went to his cabin on the 3rd floor, which housed Sales and Marketing.

At 6 pm, his phone buzzed.

"What time will you be leaving?" asked Rajeshwari.

"Another 20 minutes," he texted back.

"Ok, I'll meet you at the car in 20," she replied.

And so, it continued over the next month or two with Vikram picking her up in the morning and dropping her back in the evening. On one such ride back home, Vikram felt the need for some coffee.

"Would you care for some coffee?" he asked.

"I don't mind," she replied.

The Café Coffee Day was crowded. They found an unoccupied table in the corner. While they waited for their coffee, Vikram noticed a mark on her hand.

"Did you fall down?" he asked her.

"Oh that," she said, "is a remnant of an injury from the beating that my ex-husband had subjected me to."

"Oh, I'm sorry to hear that," he said, trying to look away and regretting yet another foot-in-the-mouth moment.

Rajeshwari continued, "I was 20 when I got married to Venkat Reddy. My father had passed away when I was just 4 years old. My mother did odd jobs to support us. Barely had I turned 18 when my mum began to press me to get married. We had no money, and Venkat was willing to marry me without any dowry. Getting married without a dowry is a big deal in our community. So, when my mother got the proposal, I was just 19, but said yes, although I was very keen to study further"

"Sir, your black coffee and latte for madam." Waiters always turn up at the wrong time.

She stirred her latte and continued, "Venkat turned out to be all things horrible. Every night he would come home drunk or, worse still, he would call his friends over and drink along with them well into the night. I was told to serve them snacks. Once they were drunk, his friends would lech and leer at me, pass comments, misbehave with me. Venkat would be too drunk to say anything or, many times, would be on his friends' side. I tried telling him several times, but it fell on deaf ears. When our arguments would get bad, he would beat me. His mother too openly sided with him. I wasn't allowed to go to meet my mother or any friends. He would keep tabs on me through his mother."

"Oh, that is so sad to hear, Rajeshwari. I wonder why he did get married in the first place if this is how he was going to treat his wife. He should have just had girlfriends and moved on from one to the other," said Vikram.

"Having a girlfriend doesn't give you the feeling of ownership, having a wife does. Guess he thought that having married me without a dowry, he owned me, and he wanted to both show and prove that to me. For him, I was nothing but a use and throw rag in his house," her eyes beginning to moisten from the memories that welled up within her. She then continued.

"One day when the beating became unbearable, I went to the police station and complained. But you know how the police are - they always side with the man. They advised us to undergo counselling, which was an exercise in futility. When I got pregnant, he said it was not his child and began to torture me. When I delivered a girl, it got even worse, with the mother-in-law now joining in and asking me to give away the child for adoption as they did not want a girl. Girls are considered a liability in our community if you are not financially well-off. My husband and my in-laws all conspired against me. I did contemplate ending our lives but didn't have the heart to kill my baby."

"That is a real plateful of problems on your hands, Rajeshwari. I'm not sure if I would have ever managed to cope with such adversity. We learn problem-solving in B School, but believe you me, nothing can prepare one for what you went through. So how did you manage to get out of that hell hole?" Vikram asked.

"Sometimes, adversity either makes you or breaks you. In this case, for my daughter's sake, I decided to fight on and just bided my time, waiting for the right opportunity. One day, when Tamannah was unwell, I took her to the doctor's and from there, took an auto and went straight to my mother's house. I have been staying there ever since. He sent me divorce papers through his lawyer, which I signed. The judge gave me full custody of my daughter. Anyways, they didn't want her," she said, tearing up.

Vikram looked at her in shock and disbelief. "That's quite a life you have had. Unfortunately, you have seen more bad than good. You have gone through so much at such a young age. Your story is one of supreme bravery in the face of insurmountable odds, truly inspirational, and I, for one, am completely in awe of how you have handled such adversity and carried on with life. Coming to think of it and on a slightly lighter note, if you could battle such odds and come out triumphant, what's a little bit of Chinese competition that me and my team can't handle? Henceforth, your story will inspire me whenever things don't go my way."

"Ha, nice of you to say that. But you know what the hardest part is? It's when someone asks me my marital status. You cannot imagine what I go through. It's better being dead than being a divorcee in our country." Her voice trailed off, and then she continued, "And the other bad part is when I see my daughter grow up without a father. When her friends at school tell her that their parents took them out on a holiday or a movie or to an amusement park and she asks me to do the same. But I can't take her because tickets are so goddamn expensive at Rs. 2000 per person to this place she wanted to go called Wonder Kingdom. I don't earn that kind of a salary to be able to afford such things."

"That I can fix," said Vikram, finishing the last of his coffee.

"I have a daughter who is the same age; we as parents can afford to give her a very privileged and pampered life. She gets everything that she wants. The least I can do is to take your daughter, who is the same age as mine, to see Wonder Kingdom. Let's do it this Saturday."

Are you sure this will be okay with your family?" she asked hesitantly.

"I won't involve my family in this. My daughter goes to Wonder Kingdom quite regularly. Besides, it will involve answering too many questions. This will be my treat to your daughter. I'll pick you up on Saturday morning at 9 at the same place."

"Are you sure… I don't want to cause a problem with your family"

"Yeah, yeah, I'm sure… shouldn't be a problem. Your daughter deserves it. Consider it as my gift to her."

∽

Wonder Kingdom was themed as an Indian Disneyland. It was about an hour's drive, on the outskirts of Bangalore, near Hosur. Children loved it, and parents would invariably end up paying quite a bit as they too would end up using all the rides along with their children. The water slides, roller coaster, dashing cars, train rides, Tamannah was in seventh heaven!

Rajeshwari wasn't comfortable after getting onto the roller coaster. She felt a bit nauseated and a bit dizzy as well. As she lost her balance, she instinctively held onto Vikram's hand.

"Are you okay? Should we sit down for a while?" he asked, realizing that the roller coaster had made her feel queasy.

"Just slightly disoriented. I'll be fine in a couple of minutes," she said.

"Don't worry, I've got your back," he said.

Post lunch, it was back to the rides and the fun. By 5 pm, they were totally exhausted and headed back home. After just about 5-10 minutes, Tamannah, who was in the rear seat, fell asleep.

"I held your hand on the rollercoaster, hope you didn't mind," Rajeshwari broke the silence.

"Mind? I quite enjoyed it," Vikram said with a mischievous wink and a smile.

"Now you're being naughty."

"Am I? I thought I was being truthful."

"Thank you for making it such a memorable day for me and my daughter."

"The pleasure is entirely mine. Don't bother, Tamanaah enjoyed herself, it made her happy, that's what we wanted to achieve, right? So, it's a successful mission," said Vikram

When they reached their destination, Vikram parked the car. Instinctively, he held her hand and kissed it.

"I'll remember this day for the rest of my life," she said as she woke up a sleeping Tamannah, bid goodbye, and walked away.

When he reached home, Janki had a quizzical look on her face. "Vikram, you've started working Saturdays now?" she asked.

"Yeah, lots of pending work and meetings," he said.

That night Vikram could barely sleep. How stupid had he acted! Why did he have to kiss her? What would she think of him? What if she complained in the office? He would lose his job, and worse still, if his wife came to know, his marriage would surely be in trouble. What had come over him?

Come Monday, after what had happened on Saturday, he did not know whether she would be there or not at their appointed place. They hadn't exchanged a text or spoken to each other since Saturday evening.

When he reached the designated place, he saw that she was there.

"I've made some breakfast for you," she said. "You can stop somewhere at a halfway point and have it. South Indian breakfast, idlis and dosas - hope you'll like it."

∽

It had been close to a year since they had first met. Over daily trips to the office, home-cooked breakfast, office parties, the odd movie, and long drives on weekends, their friendship had blossomed into love. By now, they had become almost inseparable.

Despite their best efforts to keep their affair discreet, the body language and vibes they shared were pretty apparent to all. Office gossip was hot on the topic. As happens, no one had asked them about it directly, but behind their backs, there was a lot of chatter and sniggering.

The festive season had gone well, and a sales surge towards the end of the year meant that both the annual budgeted sales and profit targets were achieved. Vikram and his team were declared the best-performing team in the Asia Pacific. To honor them, there was to be a prize ceremony at Timber Trail Resort in Chandigarh. The entire company's employees with families were to be invited. The entire resort was to be booked for two full days.

Janki had an Investor meeting to attend; Kamini had her unit tests, so both Vikram's wife and daughter couldn't attend.

He came with his parents, and Rajeshwari came with Tamannah. They all reached early in the morning. At the breakfast table, Tamannah recognized Vikram as the uncle who had taken her to Wonder Kingdom and went to his table.

"Hello, Uncle."

"Hi Tamannah, how are you?"

"I'm fine, uncle."

Vikram's parents looked at him quizzically.

"She is my colleague's daughter," he told them. "Her mother must be around somewhere close by"

"Hello," Rajeshwari had reached the table.

"Why don't you join us?" said Vikram's father. Then he looked at Rajeshwari and added, "Where's your husband? Ask him to join us as well."

"He is not here. He is in Dubai," she said.

The five of them seated at one table were further grist for the gossip mills within the company. "So now he is even introducing her to his parents," said one. "But he is married yaar, this is not right," said another. A third lady chirped in, "Arre yaar who cares these days? Her husband is in the Middle East, so she is making the most of it. And men, you know how they are, they just need a chance," she said to peals of subdued sniggers from the others.

"I would like to call Vikram to the stage, please, to honor him with the award for Best Business Manager Asia Pacific," Ed Parker, the global head for Teo Toys, was on stage to hand over the prizes.

Vikram found himself on stage to a thunderous applause as Ed handed him the trophy.

"I would like to say a big thanks to my fantastic team," he said and added, "At the half-year review, we thought we were down and out, but we picked ourselves up and went into battle with even more vigor. And as the saying goes, "God helps those who help themselves." We had headwinds in our favor, which we used, got a bit lucky, and here we are… It feels surreal and fantastic at the same time." He then called his entire team over on stage; there were celebrations all around.

Evening was when cocktails and a gala dinner were organized in an open courtyard in the resort. The entire company, all employees, were having a good time.

Vikram was there with his parents, but he couldn't find Rajeshwari. He picked up his cell phone and texted her, "Where are you?"

"In my room, will come down in 5 minutes."

"What room number are you in?"

"321"

"Wait, I'm coming in 2 minutes."

Two minutes later, the doorbell of 321 rang. She opened the door. She was in the process of changing into a saree.

"Where's Tamannah?"

"She has found some friends of her age; she must be playing with them."

"I wanted to say a big thank you to you," he said, standing extremely close to her.

"For what?" she said.

"For the great friend you have been. For being there for me every time "

"Shh," she said. "No thanks and no sorry between friends,"

He leaned forward and placed his lips on hers. He kissed her tenderly at first and then with increasing intensity. They were both fully aroused and made love. She could feel the orgasm building within her, and moments later, she came vigorously. Then he came, and they were both spent.

Barely had they finished when the doorbell rang. Both froze.

"Mummy" was the voice from outside

Vikram rushed into the bathroom.

"Coming, just a minute" she said

She opened the door, Tamannah came in

"Let's change" she said to Tamannah. "We need to go down for dinner."

The next 3 months passed by like a blur. They now lived almost like a married couple. Besides meeting up on a daily basis en route to office and back, very frequently, they would check into a hotel on a Saturday morning and check out in the evening. Sex was now quite regular and she was on the pill.

"What if you forget to take the pill and conceive?" he asked her one day.

"If it's a boy, we will name him Arya, and if it's a girl, we will name her Akanksha."

"Don't even think about it," he almost snapped at her.

∞

News of their affair had long reached the boss, but he had hoped that this was just a phase that would pass, and that he wouldn't need to intervene. After all, Vikram was his star performer and asking him to leave would rock the boat in an undesirable way. However, when he was told that l'affaire Vikram was setting a bad precedent within the organization and there could be trouble if Global HQ in Illinois got to knew of this, Debu and Sunil went into a huddle.

"If you ask me, both need to be sacked," said Debu.

"To be fair, they don't do anything indiscreet in the office. They are quite discreet about it. She doesn't report to him so there is no quid pro quo. Business performance is not being affected in any way. Whatever they are carrying on is outside of the office domain. It's a problem that should concern their families; we have no role to play in their private life. Why should it be a problem for us? Within the same department, there is a conflict of interest, but is there an HR policy in our company that forbids employees from having interdepartmental relationships?" Sunil asked.

"The entire morale of the organization has been affected by this. All that everyone is doing in the office these days is gossiping about them. This can't be good for our company's reputation or productivity. As he is senior to her, there could be legal issues as well," Debu insisted.

I can't afford to let Vikram go, why don't you ask her to go," said Sunil

"What should I say she is to be terminated for?" asked Debu.

"Find some reason. You're the HR Manager. Anyways, she has not yet completed a year so she is not a permanent employee; we can ask her to leave anytime."

A week later, Debu called her to his cabin and sacked her.

This came as a massive shock to her." I'm sorry," he had told her. "You know very well why this has happened. I did try indirectly to warn you several times, but you didn't appear to get the point."

She put her head down, went back to her desk, picked up her stuff, packed it into a carton, and left the office within 15 minutes.

Vikram was unaware of the developments. She called him on his cell phone and informed him of what had transpired. "I'm so sorry to hear this" he said. "It's really cruel of them to single you out like this. After all both of us are in this together"

"Well, you are the super-achieving, award-winning SBU head of Teo Toys. Why would they want to touch you? I'm dispensable. Use and throw, just like my ex-husband did," she said as tears began to roll down her cheeks. "I needed this job very badly; how will I survive now?"

"Don't worry, I will help you find a job in 30 days….and that's a promise" said Vikram, a steely determination writ on his face. "Just mail me your CV and leave the rest to me. And once you have found a job, I will move out of this company within the next 3 months. I don't want to work here anymore"

The next morning, her CV was in his inbox. He forwarded it to a few friends and batchmates with the right recommendations. Within 15 days, she landed her first interview and within the next 15 days, she had a job offer from Growmore Supermarkets as an Executive in their HR department. She called him to give him the news. He was delighted. After how the company had dealt with her, he figured it was just a matter of time before it would be his turn to be sacked. He knew that he had to leave before they asked him to go.

∾

Within the next 3 months, Vikram found another job as Vice President of Sales and Marketing at Atlanta Brands, an Indian company with licenses to manufacture and market several international apparel brands. His new office was at the other end of town. Since they didn't go to the same office now, meeting up had become a bit of a challenge. In her new job, Rajeshwari needed to work on Saturdays as well. The events of the past 3-4 months had also allowed Vikram to step back, ponder, and question himself. Yes, it was a fantastic feeling being in love, and

Rajeshwari was possibly just the kind of woman he desired as his soulmate, but what was the endgame this would lead to? He knew he was not being fair to his wife, but he was not being fair to Rajeshwari either. This relationship of theirs was not allowing her to move on with her life as well. She needed to re-marry and settle down. Her daughter needed to get the father she deserved. 'You are being very selfish, Vikram. You have no right to put her and her daughter through this. You don't want to rock the boat with regard to your marriage because your daughter is too precious for you. Remember, so is her daughter to her. If you truly love her, you should put a stop to this and allow her to move on with her life,' he heard an inner voice say.

One Saturday during one of their meetups, he finally spoke to her.

"We need to talk," he said.

"About what?" she asked.

"Well, about our relationship. We keep meeting about 1-2 times a month now. It's going nowhere. I can be selfish and say it's fine with me; I have a family, and I do this on the side, but I must think of you as well. You are still very young, with responsibilities of your daughter and mother. There is an entire life ahead of you. You know I love you a lot, but there is nothing I can offer you in terms of security. I feel you should look at life beyond me, move on, maybe look at getting remarried after finding a nice guy."

"So, you're done with me, is it? Had your fill and now you want to throw me out of your life? Just like your company did. Is this what it's come down to?" she said.

"No, no, don't be silly. I love you very much; a life without you is inconceivable for me, but where is all this going to lead us? I'm not planning on giving up on my marriage; however much it sucks because I can't bear to live without my daughter. So where does that leave you? Wouldn't it be better if you, too, moved on in life? What happened between us was wonderful and fantastic, and I will live with those memories for the rest of my life. The precious and intimate moments we shared, no one can take them away from us, but you seriously need to think about your and Tamannah's future. I can't give her the love that she seeks from her father. In a few years, she will grow up and begin to understand life. And most importantly, what about your future? You can't go on like this indefinitely; you need to settle down, find an anchor, and give wings to your dreams. Think about it."

Rajeshwari silently heard everything that he had to say. Tears rolled down her eyes. She didn't say a word. She knew that what she was doing didn't have societal permission, but she had loved him completely and entirely. He had made her feel alive, given her hope to live and fight on, shown her what love was all about. After the extremely unhappy experience with her ex-husband, she had developed a very negative view of life. He had come into her life and made her feel liberated, happy, and desired. And now he was calling it off. She cursed herself. Maybe she was born unlucky, maybe the sins of a past birth were catching up, maybe it was just bad karma.

"I didn't mean to hurt you," said Vikram, noticing that she was in tears and seeing that what he had said had affected her. "I just want you to think about what I've told you and reflect on it for a week, maybe two weeks, and let me know how you see things from your perspective. We can then talk about this again."

They didn't meet or communicate with each other for about 2 weeks. Then, she called. "I've been reflecting and thinking on what you told me the other day," she said. "There is this neighbor in the building that we live in. He is widowed; his wife passed away about 4 years ago. He has one son who is 5 years old. His mother and my mother have become friends. My mother had mentioned him to me about 6 months ago, but I had refused. I have decided to say yes to him now. I've told my mum about it, and they are discussing fixing a marriage date at the earliest."

Vikram was taken by surprise. He did not expect things to move this fast. "Oh! That was quite fast.... Congratulations are in order, I guess. All the very best. I will terribly miss you, of course, but as they say, life must go on and while it's going to be very tough, it is the best decision for both of us."

She didn't say a word.

He continued, "I suggest we meet up this Saturday, one final time, for a final goodbye"

The Green Habitat was where they would typically have their rendezvous. It was tucked away in a distant suburb of Bangalore, which afforded them privacy. As they sat down in the confines of their hotel room with their cell phones, deleting all the photos, mails, and texts that they had ever sent to each other, a flood of memories and remembrances came back, and they reminisced on all the great and wonderful times that they had shared together.

In a couple of hours, they were done.

"Well, that's that," said Vikram. "Guess this is the end." He switched on the TV.

Roxette was singing a song from the cult movie Pretty Woman

It must have been love, but it's over now.

It must have been good, but I've lost it somehow

He held her in his arms, and they kissed passionately. One thing led to another, and they ended up making love. A final goodbye, and each went their separate way.

Rajeshwari got married to Eknath Godbole within the next 10 days. The pandit said there was only one good mahurat date within the next 10 days, and if they missed that, they would have to wait for 6 months. Tamannah got both a father and a brother. Vikram went back to his boring, mundane corporate life.

Two Years later…:

Vikram had done well in his new assignment and had recently been promoted to COO at Atlanta Brands. Growmore Supermarkets too, had done extremely well over the past couple of years. They had opened several new outlets in Bangalore, one of which was in Koramangala, just next door to where Vikram lived.

On one lazy Sunday morning, Vikram, Janki, and Kamini had hopped across to check out the newly opened store. Each of them made a beeline to their section of interest in the store. Janki wanted to stock up on the Vegetables and Chicken; Kamini was busy checking out the chocolates and sweets, while Vikram was in the snacks section. He was busy looking at some newly launched savories, when he heard a familiar voice say "Hello Vikram"

He spun around sharply. Standing just across the aisle, he couldn't believe his eyes when he saw who it was. His heart missed a beat. "Hello Rajeshwari" he said. It had been two years since they had last met. He looked at her closely. She hadn't changed a bit. He noticed that she was wheeling a pram. He peered into the pram. There was little a baby inside who was fast asleep. "Ah, you have a baby. Congratulations" he said

"Thanks" she said

"How is your husband and Tamanaah? All good?" he asked a bit sheepishly

"Yes, all good" she said

He was in a dilemma. Should he excuse himself and leave or should he continue the conversation for a bit longer. He decided to continue

"You've come here to shop, I guess" he said

"No," she said "I've come here to collect and look at the Customer Feedback Forms. Each month I go to a different store to study the Customer Feedback. Implementing relevant Customer Feedback enhances our customer's shopping experience"

"Oh yes of course! he said "You work at Growmore isn't it?"

"Yes" she said

"Daddy, see what we got. Lots and Lots of groceries and provisions" his daughter Kamini had joined them. Soon, Janki, wheeling a shopping trolley bulging with Vegetables, Chicken and Provisions also joined them

Vikram introduced his wife and daughter to Rajeshwari and vice versa. "My wife Janki and my daughter Kamini. She is Rajeshwari, an ex-colleague from Teo Toys. Was in HR"

"Hello Rajeshwari, good to meet you," said Janki

"Hi Janki, nice meeting you as well," said Rajeshwari

Janki looked at the baby in the pram "What a cute little baby…. Is it a boy or a girl? I'm sorry but you can't tell when babies are very small."

"It's a boy," said Rajeshwari

"Peacefully asleep, isn't he? I just love that about babies. Not a care in the world. How old is he?" said Janki

"One year and three months" said Rajeshwari

"What's his name?" asked Janki

"Arya" said Rajeshwari

"Nice name," said Janki

"On the naming of the baby, I was very clear; I had mentioned this to Arya's father as well" said Rajeshwari. Then she looked at Vikram and said "If it's a boy his name would be Arya and if it was a girl her name would be Akanksha"

Karma Bites

"The Gateway of India was built by the British in 1905 as a memorial to welcome King George V to India. As you know, India was ruled by the British until 1947, and he was the King of England at the time," said Mehrunnisa, who was showing her sisters Fatima and Sana around South Bombay.

"Wow!" exclaimed the sisters in unison. "What an imposing monument… the British were really good at monument building," said Fatima.

"It took 10 years to build and needed 500 workmen who worked day and night to complete it," said Mehrunnisa, exuding elder sister vibes, eager to show off her knowledge about Bombay to her younger sisters and win their appreciation.

"Mehru apa, you are so knowledgeable. How do you know all this?" asked Sana.

"Well, you can say I am well-read," she said, exuding a 'false' air of superiority. An ice cream seller on his tricycle passed by. "Ice cream, Ice cream" he was shouting, while also intermittently ringing a small bell to attract people's attention. "Can we have some ice cream? It's so hot and humid here in Bombay," said Fatima.

"Yes, of course," said Mehrunnisa, and proceeded to buy three ice lollie's which they began slurping on.

"What's that magnificent building just opposite the road?" asked Sana, full of curiosity, completely mesmerized by the sights and sounds of Bombay.

"That, my dear, is the Taj Mahal Hotel. It was built by Jamshedji Tata, who wanted to build a 5-star hotel that would be accessible to Indians." said Mehrunnisa.

"Why? Weren't Indians allowed into 5-star hotels in those days?" asked Sana, who at 14, was the youngest of the three sisters.

"The existing luxury hotel at that time, called the Watson's Hotel, was built by the British, who would not allow Indians into it. Haven't you heard of the phrase 'Dogs and Indians not allowed'? Well, that was apparently pasted outside the Watson hotel. It was a Europeans and whites-only hotel."

"And how do you know this, Mehru apa?" Sana asked.

"This, my husband told me. We had been to the Taj for our first anniversary. He was telling me about the history of the Taj over dinner. What a fantastic hotel it is. Would you like to see it? We could have a cup of tea or coffee there, if you are interested."

"Yes, of course, we are," both the sisters chimed together.

The coffee shop at the Taj was called Shamiana. It was crowded with a mix of largely tourists and businesspeople.

Away from the noise and chatter, the three sisters found a cozy table in one corner and promptly occupied it. When the waiter came to ask them for the order, "3 cups of tea, and 3 chicken sandwiches please." said Mehrunnisa.

"Will that be all, madam?"

"Yes, please," she said.

"Wow, apa, how lucky you are," said Fatima, biting into her sandwich. "You're married here in Bombay, away from everything that we have to go through in Aligarh. Both of us have to bear the brunt of Bhaijaan's tantrums. We are treated worse than slaves in our house."

"Haven't things improved since I got married and left the house?" asked Mehrunnisa

"No, it's gotten even worse now, Apa," said Sana. "All that is expected of us is to do the housework. Cleaning, washing, cooking, and looking after the family property. When Bhaijaan gets married, we will have to look after his children. You know that we were pulled out of school when we got our periods. Girls should not go to school once they hit puberty. Who decided this? I tell you; it's a crime to be born a woman in that family."

"We live in a very traditional patriarchal family set up, Sana," said Fatima. "Bhaijaan is a tyrant. I wish our father was alive. I had heard that he was much more benevolent and supportive towards women. At least Ammi says so."

"You can also get married and escape from that house. Sana is still young but Fatima, you are 19, you can find someone, get married, and get away from that house. I managed it, you could as well," said Mehrunnisa.

"You were extremely lucky, Mehru apa," said Fatima. "Jehangir, who is a distant cousin, had come over to our house and he liked you instantly. Love at first sight, as he says when we tease him about you. He agreed to marry you without any dowry, and he also agreed to not claim any share of the family property in the future. That's the only reason why Bhaijaan agreed. What are the odds that we will be as lucky as you? That our prince charming will come on a magnificent steed, sweep us off our feet, and get married to us? Zero...."

"When will Fatima get her Jehangir?" said Sana with a mischievous smile on her face. They all cracked up.

"Madam, can I get you anything else?" the waiter came to their table and asked.

"No, that'll be all. Please get us the bill."

They exited the hotel and crossed the road. "No trip to Bombay is complete without seeing Elephanta Island," said Mehrunnisa.

Elephanta Island? What's that? asked Fatima.

"It's an island just off the coast of Bombay. It has Rock Caves with beautiful carvings cut into the rock. They are 1500 years old. A very historical and beautiful place. Less than an hour's boat ride from here. You will really like it."

"Ok, let's go!" the sisters exclaimed.

"Can you see the people queued up there? That's the queue for the tickets. We need to stand in that queue. Come on, let's queue up," said Mehrunissa

The queue was long and moved at a snail's pace. They were lost in thought, taking in the sights and sounds of the place. They did not notice a guy who had been shadowing and tailing them for some time. He was part of a chain snatchers gang that targeted unsuspecting tourists. From their behavior and movements, he had figured out that they were new to Bombay. He mingled with the crowd, quietly sneaked up on them and before they could even notice him, within the blink of an eye, he had snatched Fatima's gold chain and vanished.

Fatima's first reaction was shock. She took a good 10-15 seconds to register what had happened, after which uttered in a feeble voice "Chor, Chor, Thief, he has snatched my chain…."

"Where? Who? Someone snatched your chain. Oh God!" shrieked Mehrunnisa. Some onlookers approached them and heard her out, but did precious little. "How sad. You need to be careful, this is Bombay, not your town," said one particularly helpful person.

In some time, when they had somewhat recovered from the shock of the incident, Mehrunnisa, who had regained her composure by then, said, "We must register a complaint with the police. The Colaba police station is nearby. We have no time to lose. Come, let's go."

∽

Sub-Inspector Ramesh Nayak was seated at his desk studying a file. When he looked up, he saw three ladies seated opposite him.

"Yes, how can I help you?" he asked.

"Sir, this is my sister Fatima. We had gone sightseeing to the Gateway of India when suddenly out of nowhere, this chor, this thief, snatched her gold necklace. We have come here to register a complaint. The havildar at the gate asked us to meet you and lodge a complaint."

"Oh, okay, I'll have to ask you a few questions in order to register your complaint."

"Yes, Sure Sir"

"What's your full name?" he asked, looking towards Fatima, who was in tears and in shock after what had happened.

"Fatima Ilahi Baksh Choudhary," said Mehrunnisa.

"I haven't asked you. I'm asking her, she needs to reply," said the sub-Inspector.

He looked directly at Fatima and asked, "Your age?"

"19"

"Your address?"

"Chowdhary ki haveli, near Aligarh Fort, Aligarh 202001"

"Your address in Mumbai?"

My sister's address in Bombay, where we are staying, is

"301, Maqdoom Chambers, Bellasis Road, Nagpada,"

"Your Telephone No?"

"Aligarh: 0571-27856, Bombay: 309752"

Three days later, the phone at Mehrunnisa's house rang. "This is Sub-Inspector Ramesh Nayak from Colaba police station speaking. We have arrested a few known chain snatchers who operate in that area. Can you ask your sister to come down to the police station for an identification parade?"

"Sure," said Mehrunnisa. "She will be there in an hour."

Fatima was at the police station, seated in Sub-Inspector Ramesh Nayak's cubicle. He looked closely at her. He had liked her at first sight and wanted to get to know her better.

"Good morning. Would you like to have a cup of tea?" he asked.

"No thanks," she replied.

"So, what do you do in Aligarh?" he asked.

"I do all the housework, help out in the fields, look after my mother and my elder brother"

"And why did you come to Bombay?"

"My sister is married and lives here in Bombay," she said. "Both of us sisters come from Aligarh every year. We stay here with our sister. Shopping, sightseeing, movies, eating out... these 2-3 weeks are really a fun time for us."

"Are you married?"

"No"

"We have identified five notorious chain snatchers who operate in that area. We will show them to you one by one. I know you barely had the time to see the snatcher, but still, see if any face seems like he could be the one."

"Okay, I'll try," she said.

After the identification parade, he asked her if anyone seemed familiar.

"Not really. It all happened so fast, I can't really identify anyone with any degree of certainty" she said.

"Ok, we will try to round up a few more suspects for you to identify. I know that you didn't have much time to see his face clearly, but maybe on seeing the real culprit, something might click and you could possibly identify him."Then, after a pause, he added, "You live in Nagpada, right? I have some work there. Can I drop you home if that's ok with you?"

"That will be nice, thanks," she said.

Over the next 10-15 days or so, he kept calling her to the police station on some pretext or another. Very soon, he realized that he had completely fallen head over heels for this charming, petite 19-year-old from Aligarh who spoke with such innocence and naivety that he was completely captivated. In his heart he knew, that she was the one. Knowing that she was to return to Aligarh very shortly, he knew he had no time to waste. He was dropping her back home after another identification parade, when he popped the question "Fatima, I love you. Will you marry me?"

She was taken by complete surprise. Yes, she had met him several times over the past 10 days but had never explored or felt any romantic impulse about him. She looked at him closely. 'Not bad,' she said to herself. 'Tall and dark. Handsome? Well, not quite, but that's okay. Has a steady job? Yes. Will he ask for dowry or a share in the family property? Possibly not. Religion? That's a big problem, a dealbreaker.'

"What? How is that possible? We come from different religions; how will it work? My brother will never agree. I am sorry, but I really do not think it is possible," Fatima reacted after snapping out of the vortex of thoughts she was going through.

"I will speak to your brother," he said.

"No, you don't know him. He will not even want to speak to you. If anyone can help, it's my sister Mehru apa whom you met on the day we came to the police station to lodge a complaint. If you are truly and seriously interested in getting married to me, it's only my sister Mehru apa who can help."

"Ok, I'll speak to your sister. I am not going to take no for an answer. Once I decide on something, it gets done," said Ramesh.

"Won't happen," she said. "You don't know my brother."

"And your brother doesn't know me," he said. "I have straightened many such Bhaijaan's in my police station."

"Aligarh is not your police station. He is the king of Aligarh," she said.

"You don't know anything about me, Fatima. I come from very humble beginnings. We are a family of five comprising my mother, two brothers, and a sister. We are originally from Belgaum in Karnataka, but my father settled in Bellary many years ago. He died when I was quite young. My mum brought us up by working as a daily wage worker. She worked in paddy fields during the agriculture season and in a beedi-making factory at other times. There was never a day in which we had three square meals. Hunger and poverty have been our constant companions. When I turned 15, I came to Bombay. A distant relative of ours knew the owner of this small restaurant in Ghatkopar where I was employed as a waiter. My only salary was the breakfast, lunch, and dinner that I was given at the hotel. I've always been ambitious, had this vision that I would make it big one day. I was prepared to work as hard as needed to succeed. I enrolled and studied in a night school nearby where I completed my schooling and then completed my graduation by correspondence. There was a police station opposite the restaurant. I would go there at times to serve tea to the policemen. Seeing them in uniform, the power, the position that they wielded, fascinated me. I made up my mind to join the police force. I cleared an extremely competitive written exam followed by an equally tough physical test. Thousands apply, but only a few are selected. I've made it thus far in life purely through the dint of my hard work and confidence in my abilities. Colaba police station is my first posting. and just within 15 days, you came into my life. For me, it was love at first sight. I am convinced that we are a match made in heaven. That we are destined to be together."

Fatima was spellbound. She found his story truly inspiring. She too came from a background where she was the underdog. Different circumstances, of course, but she could clearly see and identify with him as someone who had single-handedly overcome a tough, almost hopeless situation and had come up trumps.

"Wow! That's quite a life you have had," Fatima said. "You are truly a self-made man who has come up in life the hard way. While I really appreciate and like this about you, asking my family for my hand in marriage, with you not being from a different religion, is a completely different kettle of fish. I hope you understand that."

"That we shall see," he said. "I'm willing to bet my life on the fact that you will soon be Mrs. Fatima Nayak."

"Inshallah, Ameen," she said.

A couple of days later, the doorbell rang. SI Ramesh Nayak was at Mehrunnisa's door.

"Hello, Inspector, what a surprise! Please come in and have a seat." After Ramesh was seated, she asked, "Any progress in the case, Inspector?"

"Well, our entire team is on the job. Looks like it's the handiwork of some gang who are not from Colaba. We have contacted and alerted all the police stations in Bombay. We should have a breakthrough shortly." Ramesh replied

"That's Good; thanks for all the help. Can I get you some tea or coffee?"

"Well, thanks, but it's something else that I want to talk to you about."

"What is it about?"

"About your sister Fatima. I like her and would like to marry her"

Stunned silence prevailed in the room, both unsure as to what to do or say next. Then Mehrunissa said, "Fatima did tell me about you and that you wanted to marry her. She has already told you about our elder brother, right? He is the head of our house. He makes all the decisions, and we simply fall in line. We come from a very traditional Muslim family, and for our girls to marry into another religion is unheard of. He will never allow it. You are a nice guy, and she told me she also likes you. She also told me about your background and how you were a self-made person who had battled tremendous odds to make it in life. Having said that, I really don't think getting married to her will be possible. It's better if you forget about her and move on."

"Which is why I have come to speak to you. Fatima told me that you were the only person who could speak to him and convince him……"

"For Fatima and your sake, I can try, but we already know what the result will be..."

"Please speak to him and try to convince him. Post-marriage, we will stay in Bombay. She will be close to you as well. I love her very much. Her happiness will be paramount for me. I do not want any property, dowry, or anything from your family. It's only Fatima that I wish to marry. Post-marriage, she can practice her faith, I have no issues with that," he said.

"Well, they leave for Aligarh tomorrow. I will speak to Bhaijaan in 3-4 days' time. Let's see how it goes."

"OK, thank you very much," he said, and after bidding goodbye to them, he left.

"You have done the unthinkable, Fatima, fallen in love with a policeman and that too a non-Muslim! Wow! When did this happen? So that's what all the police station visits to identify the chain chor were about? You could inspire a Bollywood director to make a movie of your love story!" Mehrunnisa teased her.

"Well, it just happened, Apa. He comes across as a very nice, simple, straightforward person. He has gone through a lot of difficulty in life to reach where he has. I don't know if it's love yet, but coming to think of it, he has a secure job, loves me very much, and getting married to him means I can stay in Bombay, near you and away from Aligarh." After a small pause, she added, "You think Bhaijaan will agree?"

"Looks tough, if not impossible, but let me try to speak to him. Let's hope for the best. I still can't believe this."

∽

"Aahh," Fatima shrieked on receiving a resounding slap on her face.

Mehrunisa had spoken to Bhaijaan, and it did not go well. Bhaijaan was extremely upset and was giving Fatima a thrashing with his leather belt.

At the end of about 30 minutes when he stopped, she was in a bad shape. Her nose and mouth were bloodied, she had belt marks all over her body. No one interfered as Bhaijaan was known to have a savage temper.

"You will never ever go to Bombay or anywhere else out of Aligarh. I will not allow you to defame the dignity and izzat of our family which we have accumulated over 400 years," he said when he was done beating her.

Her mother hugged her. "Why do you do such things, Fatima beti? You want to marry out of our religion? You should have known the consequences."

"I am not sorry, Ammi. He loves me. He will keep me happy," she said before she passed out due to the pain.

∽

"Hello, Sub-Inspector Ramesh Nayak?"

"Yes, speaking,"

"Mehrunnisa here,"

"How are you Mehrunnisa? And how is Fatima? Did you speak to your brother about us?"

"Inspector, the news I'm afraid is not too good. Bhaijaan has taken it very badly. He has beaten her black and blue. She has been barred from leaving Aligarh, and I, too, have been told to stop all interactions with you. Please don't try to call her or speak to her. She will die if they find out. We would like to withdraw the chain-snatching case. Please don't call or try to meet us again," she said, and she disconnected.

Ramesh had never seen failure in life. He believed he was destiny's child and was determined to win his love and the most important battle of his life. The odds didn't matter to him; there was no going back now. He was not going to take no for an answer. He had a plan in mind; now, it was time to execute. He went over the whole plan in his head, then picked up the phone and dialed the haveli's number in Aligarh.

"Hello," Ammi picked up the phone.

Ramesh figured that it would be her mother. "Hello, Ammi, this is Ramesh here."

"Ramesh, the policeman from Mumbai...?"

"Yes, Ammi, how are you, Ammi?"

"Why are you calling us? Don't you know the problems you have caused in our family? For God's sake, please don't call us. We have enough problems on our plate already without you causing us some more. Please leave Fatima alone. She doesn't want to talk to you," an emotional Ammi vented out in frustration and anger.

"I can understand your feelings towards me, Ammi. I just want to say one final goodbye to Fatima, and then I promise you I will never call your house or speak to anyone from your family. If you could just call her on the phone one final time. Please, I request you, Ammi," he said.

Ammi was in a dilemma. Should she disconnect the phone or let him say goodbye to his loved one final time? Bhaijaan was not at home, so there was no danger on that front. Ramesh did say he wouldn't call again, that he only wanted to say goodbye one final time. Fatima too, liked him from what she had told her. The mother's heart in her melted. "Ok," she said, "I'll get her on the phone. But as you said, this is the first and last time you will call here and speak to her."

"I promise, Ammi. You have my word," he said.

"Fatima, your phone, come here," Ammi called out to Fatima, who was in the other room washing the windowpanes.

"Who is it, Ammi?" Fatima asked as she came to the phone and placed it to her ear. Ammi left the room.

"Hello, who is this?" she asked.

"Shh, Fatima, keep quiet and only listen to what I have to say. Don't utter a word. Just disconnect the phone when I've finished speaking."

Complete silence prevailed as a startled Fatima listened to what Ramesh was saying.

Ramesh continued, "This Wednesday when you go to the market to buy groceries, a woman dressed in a burqa will meet you at Sohail Chand's shop. She will hand over to you a train ticket from Aligarh to Mumbai. The train will depart from Aligarh at twelve noon. You need to board that train. I will meet you at the VT railway station outside your compartment."

"But…"

"No ifs and no buts. If you board the train then I'll know that you love me and are interested in marrying me. If you decide not to, then to, it's fine, and I'll understand. Either way, I will always love you, Bye," said Ramesh and then hung up.

∾

Wednesday 9th May 1964 was an important date in the life of Fatima. She had made up her mind. She was going to Bombay no matter what. She was up early, had breakfast, and smuggled just a few clothes in her shopping bag. She was normally accompanied by Sana for their weekly grocery shopping but had tactfully managed and asked her not to come with her that day. As per her normal routine, she would be dropped at the market in their car. The driver would wait until she finished her shopping. The weekly groceries, meat, and all the provisions would then be filled into the car, and she would be back home by around 1 pm.

She reached Sohail Chand's shop at 11 a.m. and began shopping. The list of vegetables, tomatoes, potatoes, onions, fruit, and provisions was endless.

At precisely 11:20 am, a burqa-clad lady entered the shop, approached Fatima, lifted her veil, and said, "Hello, I am Yasmeen Bano. How are you, Fatima? Did you recognize me?" Before Fatima could react, she opened her purse, pulled out what looked like a railway ticket, pushed it into her hand, and vanished.

About fifteen minutes later, she had finished her grocery shopping. Fatima looked at the train ticket. Aligarh Jn to Bombay VT. Punjab Mail. Departure from Aligarh Jn at 12 noon. 2nd Class. Coach S4, Seat No. 15. She then looked at her watch. It was 11.35 am. The station was 10 minutes away. She walked out of the market complex and into the taxi stand. Her driver was busy gossiping with his friends over endless cups of tea and samosas. He didn't notice her slip away from Sohail Chand's shop.

At 11:50 am, she was at the railway station. She paid the taxi driver and stepped out of the taxi.

Aligarh Jn railway station was crowded. She always had her burqa on, so no one recognized her. Just as she reached platform 4, she saw the train arriving. She located her compartment and then her seat. The next 10 minutes until the train left the station were the most nerve-wracking 10 minutes of her life. If someone noticed her and informed her brother that she was on the train, it would mean the end of her life. By 12:10 pm, the train had left the station. She knew there was no going back now. She had taken the biggest (and riskiest) decision of her life in deciding to leave the house of her birth, go to another city, get married to someone she had met and barely known for 15 days. The train picked up speed. It was to reach VT station in Mumbai the next morning at 7 am. "Help me Allah, please don't forsake me," she would keep muttering to herself throughout the journey.

A pensive Ramesh was seated at his desk in Colaba police station. At 12:15 pm, he received a call from Aligarh. It was a lady's voice. "Sir, she has boarded the train."

"Thanks, Shabnam," was all he managed to say before the line disconnected.

∽

Mian Fazal reached home at around 3 pm to find commotion in the haveli.

"What happened?" he asked the driver.

"Usman Chand loaded the groceries into the car at around twelve noon and said that Fatima Bibi had asked me to wait as she was going clothes shopping in the store nearby. I waited for 2 hours and then came back home. I searched everywhere, including the ladies cloth stores, but she was not to be found," said the driver, on the verge of breaking down.

"Ok, I'll ask some friends in the city who live near the market area to look around. If we can't trace her or she doesn't return in 1-2 more hours, we will file a missing person police complaint," said Bhaijaan looking grim and worried.

∽

The Punjab Mail had a reputation for being on time. 7 am sharp and it chugged into VT station. The passengers began to get off the train. Fatima was one of the last to exit. She looked up and down but didn't find Ramesh. The first pangs of anxiety began to hit her. Had she been tricked? What if Ramesh didn't show up? What if her worst fears came true? She was lost in thought when she felt a tap on her back. She looked around and saw Ramesh. Instantly she leapt into his arms, a feeling of both pure joy and relief engulfing her.

"This, my dear, is going to be home for us for the next few weeks, maybe months," Ramesh had taken her to his twin-sharing bachelor's accommodation at the police quarters in Colaba. "I share this room with another colleague, SI Rane, but he has graciously moved to the other room which he will now share with two others. I have already applied for family quarters, and I've been told it should be done in a few weeks. Inspector Godbole, the Inspector in charge, has put in a strong word. Meanwhile, you can freshen up, have a shower, we will grab some breakfast and then go to the marriage registrar's office where we have been given a time slot of 1 pm to register our marriage."

At the registrar's office, things went off smoothly. All the background paperwork had already been done by Ramesh. His two colleagues, SI Rane and SI Sanap, were the witnesses.

By 2pm on the 10th of May 1964, they were declared man and wife. To celebrate their marriage, they went for lunch to Khyber restaurant at Kala Ghoda. There was just one thing left to be done. She had to call her sister, and Ramesh had to inform his family.

"Hello Mehru apa," Fatima had very nervously picked up the phone and called her sister. "Where have you been, Fatima? They are looking high and low for you in Aligarh. Bhaijaan has filed a missing person complaint at Aligarh police station. Thank God you are safe."

"I called to tell you that I am in Mumbai and have got married in a civil court to Ramesh"

"You've done what? Are you out of your mind? If they get to know that you have run away from home and got married in secret, all hell will break loose. Bhaijaan will kill you for sure. I won't tell anyone. Please go home immediately."

"I've taken this decision Mehru apa, for right or for wrong it's my life now. If you could please inform them in Aligarh. If I call, they won't understand, and things could get even worse"

"I will call them and inform them, of course, but you understand that this could be the end of your association with the family."

"For now, yes, but time is a great healer. Who knows what fate has in store for us?" Fatima's voice had a steely determination to it.

"I think you are making a big mistake, Fatima. It's not too late, even now. You will be cutting off all ties with your family and entrusting your whole life to a stranger you hardly know. How do you know he will take care of you and won't abandon you once his carnal desires are satisfied? I will say that you came to my house in Mumbai because you were mentally disturbed. Everything will be forgotten and forgiven. No one will know. Please return to Aligarh," she pleaded.

"No, Apa, that ship has sailed. That bridge has been crossed. Now, it's my destiny and Allah's will. I have great faith in Allah. He will protect me," Fatima said.

"Well, it appears that you have made up your mind. All I can do is wish you all the best for your married life. You are taking a massive risk. I hope things work out for you, my dear sister, because if they don't, then jumping under a train will be the only option left for you. Goodbye and good luck!" Mehrunnisa said and then disconnected.

∾

Bhaijaan got the news. He was furious. Fatima had spoiled the family name, and he was going to make her pay. Since Ramesh was a policeman, threatening him or trying to get him beaten up by using goons was going to be difficult. He summoned his lawyers to see what legal options he had.

"We wouldn't advise filing a kidnapping case," the lawyers told him. "She is above eighteen and has gone to Bombay of her own will. They have got married in court. The judge will dismiss the case in the first hearing itself."

But Bhaijaan was not one to give up so easily. By hook or by crook, he wanted to teach her a lesson. She had spoiled the family name and wasn't going to allow her to live in peace. He knew of a fakir who practiced black magic. All he needed to do was to give him the photograph of the person on whom he wanted the spell to be cast.

"I've read the spell," the Fakir told him. "It will affect either her or the person she loves the most. If it works optimally, one of them will die."

"I can't understand what's going on" Dr. Tibrewala was telling Fatima. Ramesh had been admitted to the police hospital for the past week. "He has been suffering from a mystery fever for the past 10 days which we are not able to diagnose. All the tests done on him seem to come out negative. He slips in and out of a coma. We have tried everything but nothing seems to work."

Fatima had heard of the magical powers of prayers made at the Haji Ali dargah. She was there early next morning. "Allah, please save my husband. If you feel that I have done anything wrong that is against your principles, please punish me, but spare him. Your devotee begs for his life. If anything were to happen to him, I would have nowhere to go and would end my life here in this dargah by jumping into the sea."

Two days later, the fever began to come down. A week later, Ramesh was discharged, and after a week of rest at home, he was back at work.

∾

Indira Gandhi declares, "Land to the tiller - A massive social reform," screamed the May 21, 1966 edition of the Times of India. It was her idea of redistributing the wealth in the country, which was until then in the hands of a few feudal elites. At one stroke, all the landlords who owned vast tracts of property had to surrender their land to those who worked on their farms. The Chowdhury family was no exception. From owning 50 acres of land, they were left with just the haveli over the next 2-3 years.

The family's earnings, which were totally dependent on the revenue from the crops and plantations grown on their property, had reduced considerably. From living a luxurious life, they were now financially in bad shape.

News from Aligarh kept trickling into Fatima from friends and well-wishers. Bhaijaan had gotten married in 1965 and by the spring of 1968 had become a father to two children. An elder daughter Nafeesa and the younger, a boy called Salim.

Fatima was pregnant and due to deliver early next year.

27th February 1969 was a massive day for Ramesh and Fatima. They had become proud parents to Akash. "Your son will be bright, intelligent and bring great name to your family," said the astrologer when he was done preparing his horoscope.

21 years later...:

As predicted, Akash did well at school and college both academically and in sports with a keen interest in physics and math. By May 1990, Akash had completed his graduation and had obtained admission to Purdue University in the US to do his Masters in Electronic Engineering. The family decided to have a short holiday in Goa before he left for the US. They were booked at the Bogmalo Beach Resort in Goa.

"Hello Ramesh, sorry to disturb you on your holiday." It was the Commissioner of Police, Bombay on the phone.

"No problem, sir. Once in uniform, there is no Sunday and no holiday," both cracked up.

"We have information from intelligence that the notorious criminal Charles, who fled from Tihar Jail, is holed up in Goa and will be going to have lunch tomorrow at a restaurant called O Coqueiro in Calangute, Goa," the commissioner said before he paused and continued.

"He is apparently in disguise, but I know that you have interrogated him in the past in connection with a murder case, and you know what he looks like."

"Yes, sir, I know Charles very well," said Ramesh.

"A team comprising of eight fully armed commandos is already in Goa. All they want is for you to identify Charles and then they take over."

"Noted Sir," said Ramesh.

"Please call and meet ACP Madhukar Bhende within an hour. He is heading the Operation. You will find him at the

Calangute Police Station. He will brief you further. Best of luck, Ramesh. Goodbye."

"Something urgent has come up, I'll be back shortly," said Ramesh to his wife and son.

"But I thought we were on a holiday, dad! This is supposed to be family time. What kind of a job is this? Are there no Sundays or holidays in your job?"

"I think you overheard me speak with the commissioner, for a policeman, there is no Sunday and no holiday. Relax, I'll be back in a couple of hours," he said and quickly got dressed, stepped out of the hotel, and hailed a taxi.

It was about half an hour from his hotel to the Calangute Police Station. Ramesh cast his mind back to the time when he had interrogated the international fraudster and criminal Charles. Taking to a life of crime was the easiest thing for him. He would befriend young women, win their confidence, promise marriage, take all their money, and then murder them. He had been arrested by the Colaba police station in 1973 in connection with the murder of a prostitute but was let off for lack of evidence. He was a wanted man in Thailand as well where he had committed a series of murders.

The O Coqueiro restaurant and bar had a reputation for serving authentic Goan food. It was a magnet for foreigners and tourists and was located on the main highway that connected Mumbai (Bombay had since been renamed) with Goa. There was information that Charles, along with three of his accomplices, would be coming for lunch at around

2 pm. ACP Bhende and his team had already surveyed the place and placed armed commandos at strategic places.

At 2.15 pm, Ramesh saw three people enter the restaurant. One of them was bearded with a thick mop of hair. He had a slight limp. Ramesh recognized him instantly. He allowed them a couple of minutes to settle in and then walked to their table and said,

"Hello Charles, do you recognize me?"

"Er, I'm afraid I don't," Charles was dismissive.

"I arrested you in 1973 in connection with a murder.... recall anything, Charles?"

Charles tried to reach for his revolver, but it was too late. The two commandos seated at the adjoining tables pounced on him and pinned him to the ground. His two other accomplices tried to flee but were apprehended by the commandos who were waiting outside. The operation was a grand success. Inspector Bhende got all the credit for leading the team, but Ramesh's role in identifying Charles and in doing so, risking his life, was praised in the highest quarters.

In September 1990, Ramesh was given the President's Medal for Gallantry.

In 1991, he was promoted to Assistant Commissioner and made head of the Anti-Narcotics Cell.

Within a year of his appointment, Ramesh busted several drug-running gangs across the city and earned the nickname "Drug Buster" due to his exploits and successes.

A year later, in one of the meeting rooms at the Mumbai Police Headquarters in Crawford Market, Ramesh was being briefed by his intelligence team.

"Sir, we have information about a certain 'Rocket Gang' based out of Aligarh as the kingpin of the narcotics flowing into Mumbai."

"Fazal Ilahi Choudhary alias Bhaijaan heads the gang. They used to own lots of property in Aligarh at one time. After their properties were taken over by the government, they were left with practically no land. The family saw bad days. Choudhary then hatched a plan with those very farmers to whom his lands were given. Instead of growing paddy and wheat, he told them, 'You can grow poppy. I will give you five times the price that you get for paddy and wheat.'

He then set up a factory to convert the poppy into charas, ganja, opium, and various other drugs. He created various syndicates and middlemen through whom he sells these drugs at huge prices in big cities like Mumbai, Delhi, and Bangalore. He is coming to Mumbai next week to do a big deal worth several crores with the local gangs here. We hear Salim Langda of the D Company will be meeting up with him. Once we get the location of where they plan to meet, we need to strike."

There was pin-drop silence in the room for the next couple of minutes as Ramesh tried to make sense of all that he had heard. Then he stood up and spoke

"I will lead this operation. This is much more than a drugs bust. It's personal."

Lost and Found

Part 1: Mumbai - Maharashtra:

"Where are you going, Ajji?" Kushal, all of 10, asked his grandma.

"I'm going to the hospital, beta. My health is not very good. Maybe it's just old age. The doctor has asked me to undergo a whole series of tests to identify what's wrong with me," she replied.

"Where is this hospital, Ajji? Can I come with you, please?"

"No, beta. I will be undergoing many tests there. X-ray, blood tests, ECG, etc. I'll be shuttling from one room to another, from one floor to another. You will be left all alone. The doctors won't allow you to accompany me. Who will take care of you? And the hospital is in Sion, it's quite far away from Vikhroli."

"Ajji, please...."

"Now, don't be stubborn, beta, please listen to your Ajji. I'll be back soon; it's just a matter of 4-5 hours."

Kushal began to cry. "I want to come with you Ajji...." he wailed

Kushal's father Suhas, who had been overhearing the grandma-grandson conversation, intervened. "Kushal, why are you crying and creating all this commotion? Stop throwing tantrums. Don't you understand that you cannot go along with Ajji to the hospital? It's not a park or a playground. She is going for her medical tests and will be back soon. Learn to listen to your parents and elders."

"Why are you shouting at the poor child? You know he loves his grandma and can't live a moment without her. He is only a child, let him be," said Kushal's mother, Meena, who was in the bedroom feeding Kaushalya, their 6-month-old baby.

"He is not a child; he is 10 years old for heaven's sake. Both you and your mother have spoiled him rotten. He behaves more like a 4-year-old. Look at our neighbour's child Ganpat who is all of 8. See how mature he is for his age," said Suhas.

Kushal sat in a corner, head down, and in a sulk. Realising that he was upset, his grandma tried to cheer him up: "Every child is different. Some mature early and some remain childlike even into their teens and twenties. Besides, he will always remain a child for me, isn't it, Kushal? Don't you worry, beta, I'll be back in a jiffy and as a special treat for my special grandson, on my way back, I will get for you your favourite shrikhand."

"Aaee, I would have dropped you at the hospital, but I need to go out for some urgent office work," said Suhas.

"No problem, I will manage. I've been there before. I'll take an auto to Vikhroli station, then the train to Sion station, and from there it's a 10-minute walk to the hospital. I'll be fine, really. You please carry on," Ajji said.

Kushal heard the door shut. He looked up. His father had stepped out of the house. Ajji was ready to leave as well. He tried one final time, "Ajji, can I come with you? I won't give you any trouble, I promise..."

"No, beta, you can't come with me. Stay put at home and do your homework. I'll be back before you even know it." She said a final goodbye to him, opened the door, stepped out of the house, and shut the door behind her.

Kushal tiptoed into the bedroom. His mother and little baby sister were fast asleep. He looked out of the window and saw Ajji hail an auto. He made up his mind. 'I'll be all by myself for the next 4-5 hours. It'll be so boring. Won't it be great if I follow Ajji to the hospital and surprise her?' he told himself. He then crystallised his thoughts a bit further. 'Ajji will never be angry with me. As for baba, he is always angry with me and says I'm immature. By going out alone to Sion Hospital, I can prove to him that I am not immature and can handle myself.'

Decision made, he quietly changed into his jeans, wore his favourite t-shirt, and put on his sandals. From his piggy bank, he took out all the coins and filled them into his pockets. One final glance into the bedroom to recheck on his mother and baby sister. He then opened the door with the minimum of noise, stepped out of the house, and shut the door behind him.

The building watchman saw him leave the main gate.

"Where are you going, beta Kushal?" he asked.

"My grandma forgot her glasses at home. She can't see very well without her glasses, so she called and asked me to get them. She is waiting for me at Vikhroli station," Kushal said.

"Do you want me to accompany you?" he asked.

"No," said Kushal, "I'll be fine. Don't worry."

"Ok beta," he said and opened the main gate of the building. He helped Kushal in hailing an auto and told the autowallah, "Please drop him at Vikhroli station." Kushal got into the auto, and the watchman saw it melt away into the dense Mumbai traffic.

∾

"Sahab, our son has been missing since this afternoon. We have checked with all our relatives and his friends; he is not there. Please search for him and find him, Sahab. He is my only son. I will die without him," a wailing and inconsolable Meena, accompanied by Suhas, was seated opposite Inspector Gaitonde the officer in charge at the Vikhroli Police station.

"Don't cry, madam. Crying won't help. I assure you; we will do our best to find him. But before we start investigating the case, I need to ask you a few questions…"

Over the next hour or so, Suhas gave Inspector Gaitonde the entire background of Kushal, his attachment to his grandmother, what had transpired in their house that morning, and what the watchman had told him when he had inquired about Kushal.

"So, it appears that Kushal was upset because you refused to allow him to accompany his grandma to the hospital. Seeing that no one was at home, and his mother was fast asleep, he decided to go there by himself."

"Yes, Inspector, it looks like that's what has happened," said Suhas.

The Inspector looked at Meena. She was distraught, in tears, and unable to talk coherently.

"Are you carrying any photographs of Kushal?" he asked Suhas.

"Yes, Inspector." said Suhas as he handed over 2 photos of Kushal.

"Do you have any other identification card... like say an Aadhaar?"

"Yes, Inspector, we have just recently got his Aadhaar card done. Here it is."

"Ok, that's all I need for now," said the Inspector. He then pressed a call bell on his table. A constable entered his cabin and gave him a crisp salute.

"Salunkhe, we are looking for a 10-year-old boy who has left his home in Vikhroli to go to Sion Hospital and has gone missing en route. We know for certain that he has taken an auto from their building to Vikhroli station. He would have most probably planned to take the train from Vikhroli to Sion. Check for CCTV camera feed from twelve noon on the entire route. Phone the railways and check if they have custody of a 10-year-old boy with them. This is his photograph. Send one sepoy by train from Vikhroli station to Sion and then let him go to the hospital and inquire at the hospital and surrounding areas as well."

"Yes, sir," said the constable, gave the Inspector another starchy salute and left the room.

"Don't worry, I can understand what you are going through. We will leave no stone unturned in trying to find your son. There is also the possibility that he may have realised his mistake in leaving the house and gone into hiding, worried and scared about how his father will react," said Inspector Gaitonde to the parents.

"I had told him several times not to be harsh on the child," said Meena, speaking in between sobs. "Now look at the tragedy that has befallen us."

Suhas put his head down and didn't say a word.

∾

"That's Vikhroli railway station," said the auto driver, pointing to the entrance of the station, just as he parked the auto.

"Thank you, *Bhaiiya ji*," said Kushal. "How much is it?"

The auto driver looked at the metre. "Twenty-five rupees," he said.

Kushal showed the driver all the coins he had taken from his piggy bank. "Will that be enough?" he asked.

"That's two rupees less."

"Oh! that's all I have, *Bhaiyya ji*"

"OK, that's fine. Next time your parents send you to Vikhroli station to run an errand, tell them to give you enough money."

"I will tell them for sure, *Bhaiyya ji*. Thank you."

Vikhroli station was crowded. This was the first time that Kushal was out in a public place, all by himself. He looked at the sea of people and was uncertain of what to do next. To his left, he noticed an elderly gentleman. "Uncle, how do I get to Sion?" he asked rather hesitantly.

"Beta, you want to go to Sion?"

"Yes Uncle"

"Are you alone? Is there no one with you?"

"No Uncle, I am alone"

"Haven't had a fight with your parents and run away from home, have you?"

"No, Uncle, I'm going to Sion Hospital to meet my grandma."

"That's very sweet of you, beta. These days, where do grandchildren care for their grandparents?" Then after a bit of a pause, he added, "To get to Sion, you need to catch a train from platform 2. See this staircase there? You need to climb it, then take the first right and descend those stairs. It gets you onto platform 2." He then looked at an indicator and said, "The next train comes in 7 minutes."

"OK Uncle, I'll get to platform 2."

"Do you have a ticket?"

"No uncle"

"Come with me, I'll get you a ticket," said the uncle. He took Kushal to the ticket vending machine and punched a few buttons on the touchscreen. In a few seconds, a ticket popped out. He placed it in Kushal's hand. "There you go," he said. "Now you better hurry, there are only 3 minutes for the train to come."

"Thank you, uncle," said Kushal and disappeared into the crowd.

∽

At around 6.15 pm, Meena and Suhas returned home from the police station to find Ajji sprawled on the floor.

"Aaee," screamed Meena. She put her finger under her nostrils and tried to find a pulse or a heartbeat. She found none. "I don't think she is breathing. Suhas, please call the doctor, quick," she said.

Suhas dialed their family doctor from his cellphone. "Doctor," he said, "My mother-in-law is lying unconscious on the floor. Looks like she has suffered a heart attack."

"Do you know how to administer CPR?"

"No doctor"

"Call an ambulance. Until then, don't move her. I'll be there in 10 minutes," said the doctor.

10 minutes later, the doctor arrived. He examined her and then gravely declared, "I'm afraid she is no more."

∾

"Next station, Sion," said an announcement on the train's PA system. At Sion station, Kushal disembarked. 'Now it should be easy. From what Ajji was saying, it's just a 10-minute walk to the hospital.' he told himself.

"Uncle, which is the way to Sion Hospital?" he asked a passerby. "First right, you'll get to a junction; at the junction, take the second right, then the first left and the hospital will be right in front of you," said the passerby.

He stepped out of the station. He followed the instructions, or so he thought. Thirty minutes later, instead of being in front of Sion Hospital, he found himself lost in the labyrinths of Dharavi, also known as Asia's largest slum. He tried asking people the way out, but the more directions he received, the more confused he got. Finally, by 6 pm, around the same time as his beloved grandma breathed her last, he broke down and began to cry.

A crowd of onlookers gathered around him. "Why are you crying?" asked one. "I'm lost," he said through his sobs. "I want to go to my Ajji and my parents." "Where do you stay?" asked another. "Vikhroli," he said, struggling to speak through his tears. "That's quite far away. How did you reach here?" said another. Kushal began to cry even harder.

Some of the ladies who had gathered there began to cluck. One of them said, "How sad, the poor child is lost. I wonder where he is from and how he got here. His parents must be so worried about him…" Amidst all this, a saree-clad lady came forward, held Kushal's hand, and said, "I will take you home, beta, don't worry."

Kushal looked at her. She had a very kind face. Her demeanor reminded him of his mother. Kushal instinctively hugged her. "Thank you, aunty," he said.

"But first, let's eat something; you must be terribly hungry, my child," she said. The crowd dispersed. The lady held his hand and took him to her room. It was a small 10ft x 10ft shanty, with a bed in a corner and a makeshift kitchen with some utensils lying strewn around.

"Sit down," she said, indicating the bed. "What's your name, beta?" she asked.

"Kushal," he said.

Oh! That's a nice name! And what would you like to eat?"

"Maggi noodles," he instinctively answered. Kushal loved Maggi noodles; it was his favourite snack.

I don't think we have Maggi noodles at home, beta. Can I make you something else? What else do you like? Do you like Kande-Poha?

"I like Poha too."

15 minutes later, she served him the most delicious Poha with some biscuits and tea.

Kushal was quite hungry by now. He gobbled it all up in a jiffy. Once he was done, he asked her, "Aunty, what's your name? Is this your house?"

"My name is Rukmini. This is my sister's house. I had come here just for two days to visit her. My house is far away from here. It's in a town called Raichur in Karnataka. It's a beautiful place. I have two daughters, Ayushi who is six and Khushi who is four. You will enjoy playing with them. Would you like to come with me to my house?"

"Yes, aunty, I would love to. But what about my parents? We need to inform them. They will be worried about me. They don't know that I have left home to visit my grandma in Sion Hospital."

"Don't worry, beta, I will take care of that. You must be very tired. Have a bath, I'll serve you dinner, and then, you go to sleep. We will leave for Raichur tomorrow morning by the 8 am train."

An hour later, dead tired with all his peregrinations, Kushal drifted off to sleep,

In some time, there was a knock on the door. Rukmini opened the door. It was her sister, Kadambari.

"Hello Rukmini Akka, how was your day?" she asked. Her gaze then shifted to the boy sleeping on the floor. "Who is this boy, Akka?"

"That is the son that I always wanted and never had," Rukmini replied.

"What do you mean, Akka?"

" After my second daughter was born, the doctors said that due some problem with my uterus, I will not be able to bear any more children. Can you believe my luck! The poor child followed his grandma to hospital, got lost, and landed up here in the slums of Dharavi. I see it as God answering my prayers to give me the son that I always wanted. Tomorrow morning, we leave for Raichur. Both our lives will change forever.

Part 2: Raichur - Karnataka:

The Mumbai-Bangalore Udyan Express chugged into Raichur Station at 9 pm, an hour late.

"Wake up, Kushal beta, we have reached," said Rukmini.

Kushal rubbed his eyes as he woke up. Rukmini held his hand as they disembarked from the train. A short auto ride later, he found himself at Rukmini's house.

Devaiah, her husband, was not home yet. Ayushi and Khushi, her two daughters were at the door, all excited to see her.

"Mummy," they said in unison as they hugged her. "What have you got for us from Mumbai? And who is this boy?"

"That is your brother, his name is Kushal. Say hello to him."

"Brother?" asked Ayushi, looking very surprised

"Yay, we have a brother, we have a brother," chimed little Khushi.

"He is older than both of you. Call him Anna," said Rukmi.

"Hello Anna," both the girls said in unison.

"Hello," said Kushal, still trying to take in his new surroundings.

"We have had a long and tiring day. Let's grab some dinner quickly and hit the bed as soon as we can. Kushal will sleep in your room," said Rukmini.

Close to midnight, Rukmini heard a knock on the door. She opened the door. The whiff of alcohol pervaded through the room. "I have told you so many times not to drink so much," she hissed.

"Aye, you bitch, stop lecturing me, understood! I will do whatever I want. Nobody can stop me. I drink with my own money, not yours."

"Yes, we know that. I work as a daily wage earner in the factory nearby. Whatever I earn goes towards our food and daily expenses. If you didn't spend your money on booze, we could have given our children a good education. And now there is Kushal as well we need to look after…"

"Kushal? Who is this Kushal? Some new guy you are sleeping with?"

"Have some shame. He is a little boy, maybe about 8-10 years old. He was lost in Mumbai. I got him along with me. He will stay with us from now onwards. He will complete our family; he will be the son that we didn't have."

"What have you done, you stupid woman? You have brought someone else's child into our home? Do his parents know? I am sure his parents have filed a missing person report. Do you realise this could be considered as kidnapping, and we could both end up in jail?"

"How will anyone know? It's not as if too many people come to our house anyway."

"I will inform the police myself tomorrow morning. This is too risky. I don't want to spend the rest of my life in jail. You can go to jail if you wish to." Devaiah snarled at her.

"Shh! Quiet! you will wake up the kids. No one is going to jail. He will be our son, Devaiah, think about it. I can't bear any more children. Don't we need a son to carry forth your family name?"

"Yes, but to do so by kidnapping someone's child…"

"I haven't kidnapped him. He has come of his own. Ask him if you don't believe me"

"Where is he?"

"He is sleeping in the other room. I've laid out the mattress on the floor for him."

Devaiah went to have a look. He saw that the boy was fast asleep.

"I can't agree to this. Let's go to the police tomorrow. We will tell them that you found him abandoned at the railway station and that he just tagged along with you. Let's not do this, Rukmini. Trust me, I have a bad feeling about how this will end."

"Don't worry, you are unnecessarily getting stressed," she said. Then she held his hand, pulled him towards her, and kissed him tenderly on his lips. "You need to get rid of all that stress, dear," she said as he put his hand on her breast. She noticed the bulge in his pants grow. They quickly undressed, made love, and then drifted off to sleep.

A week into staying at his new home, and after the novelty of being in a new place had worn off, Kushal began to miss home. "Aunty, is there a phone at your house? Did my parents or grandma call? I miss them, I would like to go back home."

"Don't worry, beta, I have informed them. They are fine with you coming here," she said.

"But you don't even allow me to go out of the house. I would like to go out and play cricket with the boys who play in the fields."

"You are new to this place. These boys from the village are up to no good. You can play with your sister's, right?" Kushal wasn't convinced. He broke into a sulk. "Ok, here's what we will do. I will make you some Maggi noodles and then let's all four of us play a game of 'Chor Police'."

And so, it continued over the next month or so. Rukmini kept trying to create an environment where Kushal would forget his home and accept them as his new family, but Kushal kept getting more and more homesick. "You can call me mummy beta; I'm just like your mother, isn't it?" she asked him one day. "You are my aunty," he had said to her. "My mother lives in Mumbai and I miss her very much."

An urban kid, living in this semi-rural environment, was not something he was used to. Devaiah kept his distance from him, unsure of where all of this would lead to. Little Khushi had no problem accepting him as her brother and was quite friendly towards him, Ayushi wasn't as welcoming. She was used to being the elder sibling, and now she had competition thrust upon her.

Two months later, Kushal's patience ran out. He made up his mind that he needed to escape from the house and head back to his home, to his parents, to his Ajji in Mumbai. He did broach the topic with Aunty Rukmani several times, but each time she changed the topic and put it off. He knew she would not allow him to go back of her own volition, and that he would need to do something himself.

He had observed that there was a set daily pattern for 6 days of the week. Rukmini and Devaiah would both go to work early in the morning and return in the evening. At 9 am, Ayushi would go to school. He would be all alone at home with Khushi until Ayushi came back from school, which was around 1 pm. The three of them would have lunch that Rukmini had cooked in the morning.

He figured that his best chance of escaping was when Ayushi had left for school and Khushi was busy playing with her toys in her room. On a Thursday morning, at around 11 am, he spotted his chance, packed a few clothes in his bag, opened the main door without any noise, and ran as fast as he could.

It was around twelve noon when he reached the railway station. It was not very crowded. He saw a porter and approached him, "Excuse me, uncle, where does the train for Mumbai leave from?"

"You're going to Mumbai? All by yourself? No one to accompany you?"

"My uncle is meeting me at the station," he said. "He told me to meet him on the platform where the train to Mumbai leaves from."

The porter looked at him, not very convinced by his explanation. He hesitated a bit before looking at the kid again and said, "The Chennai-Mumbai express arrives at platform no. 3 in 20 minutes. Climb up the stairs you see here and then descend the stairs from there. That's platform 3 over there. Can you see it?"

"Yes, I can. Thank you very much, uncle," said Kushal, and he sped off.

He climbed up and then down the flight of stairs just as he was told. Platform 3 wasn't very crowded. He found an empty bench and sat on it, waiting for the train to come. He was lost in thought, wondering about what would happen when aunty found out that he had run away. He didn't hear the announcement on the PA system in Kannada followed by Hindi and then English. "Passengers kindly note a change in platform. The 22160 down Chennai-Mumbai express will now be arriving on platform 2. The 22159 Up Mumbai-Chennai Express will now be arriving on platform 3."

Just as the porter had said, within 20 minutes, the train arrived on platform 3. He boarded it, found an empty seat, and promptly occupied it. When the train moved out of the station, he had a feeling of relief, 'Finally, I'm going to get back to Mumbai. What a surprise it will be for my parents and Ajji. I hope baba won't be too angry with me.' he told himself. The train moved out of the station and picked up speed. The breeze across his face and the rocking train movement made him feel sleepy. In no time, he had drifted off to sleep, telling himself that when he woke up, he would be in Mumbai.

∽

Inspector Gaitonde was in the middle of a crime control meeting when his phone rang. He picked up the call.

"Inspector, sorry to disturb you, but is there any news on our Kushal?"

"We are trying, Suhas. We know for a fact that he reached Sion station and got down there. He can be seen exiting the railway station. After that, the CCTV footage seems to have gone cold. We have made inquiries at all the adjoining places like Dharavi, Matunga, Chuna Bhatti. No one seems to have seen him. Our men are looking for him in all the possible places that we think he could have possibly gone to, but so far, we have drawn a blank. Hope to give you some good news soon."

"I don't know if you are aware of this, but his grandmother passed away the very day we came to the police station. His mother doesn't keep very good health. She has turned into a recluse, keeps talking to herself. She has been prescribed antidepressant medication. Please help us, Saheb, you are our only hope."

"Sorry to hear that, Suhas. I've told you. I will try my best. Must get off this call now, as I'm in the middle of a meeting," said the Inspector.

Part 3: Tirupati - Andhra Pradesh:

Kushal was fast asleep when he heard "Ticket please," a voice that sounded to him like it was in the far distance. He then felt someone shaking him. He snapped out of his sleep. "Have we reached Mumbai?" he asked the person who was standing next to him.

"Mumbai? Looks like you got onto the wrong train, beta. Are you travelling alone? Where are your parents?"

"Is this station not Mumbai?" he asked again.

"No, it's Tirupati,"

"How far is Mumbai from here?"

"It's very far from here. You need to board another train to go to Mumbai. Looks like you boarded the wrong train." said the TC

Kushal began to cry. "I want to go to Mumbai to meet my parents and my Ajji" he wailed.

The TC was a kind soul. "I'll help you get there," he said. "But first, you need to get down from this train."

Once they had disembarked, he said to him, "You must be hungry, right? I'll get you some tea and something to eat."

Kushal was famished. He gulped down the idlis and tea that the TC had got for him.

The train honked. It was ready to leave. "Beta, this train leaves in one minute. I am the TC on that train. I need to be on it. I will hand you over to the policeman you see there. He will help you in getting to Mumbai. Don't worry, you will be fine," he said and then went over to meet the policeman. Both had a quick chat, following which the TC boarded the train. The train honked and chugged out of the station.

The policeman looked at Kushal.

"How come you're alone? Did you run away from home?" he asked.

"I want to go to Mumbai," he said. "My parents and Ajji live there."

"I can't take you to Mumbai," the policeman said. "Look, as per the protocol that we must follow, for kids who are lost, we must take them to the nearest children's home.

There you will have to wait for your parents to get in touch with you through the proper channel."

"I want to go home" said Kushal on the verge of tears

"Come with me," the policeman said as he held Kushal's hand and walked out from the railway station onto the busy street.

The Children's Shelter Tirupati wore an old and dilapidated look. The facade showed clear signs of wear and tear. It hadn't been maintained or painted in ages. Crumbling plaster and broken masonry greeted Kushal and the policeman as they entered the office. An elderly man in horn-rimmed glasses manned the desk in the reception.

"Found this boy at the station, says he is from Mumbai," said the policeman.

"Did you run away from home after a fight with your parents?" asked the man at the desk.

Kushal didn't say a word.

"He seems very frightened. Please keep him in the shelter while we try to communicate with the Mumbai Police and try to find his family. We will also update the missing children register on the national database. If a missing person complaint has been lodged by his parents, it will be picked up."

"There is no room here. You will need to try elsewhere," said the man at the desk after going through a thick register.

"Please sir, I am requesting you. Where will the poor child go in this city? Try and see what you can do, sir," said the policeman.

He looked at the policeman and then at Kushal. "Only because I have known you for 2 years, and since you insist, I will try. Meanwhile, please fill in this form."

"Thank you, sir," said the policeman and left.

Formalities completed, Sudhakar took him inside the building to where the kids lived. The shelter housed about 200 kids, almost all of them either abandoned by their parents, or those whose parents had died and had nowhere to go. There were two sections - one for girls and one for boys. Typically, children between the ages of 7-18 were admitted. Some had criminal cases against them. For those who knew the "system" well, they could smuggle in cigarettes, alcohol, some even did drugs. The home provided three meals a day and a place to sleep for the night. There was a giant room in which everybody lived. At night, they were given flea and bug-infested mattresses to sleep on. Lunch and Dinner comprised of watery dal, half-cooked chapatis, rice which at times was worm-infested. Occasionally, on festivals like Pongal, they would have the luxury of kheer *or payasam.*

There were rites of initiation for newcomers. Ragging, which in an extreme case could lead to sodomy, was rampant. It was an extremely intimidating cauldron of an atmosphere that Kushal walked into.

The man at the reception then took Kushal into a large hall where all the children were hanging around. "Everybody, this is Kushal, he is from Mumbai. He got lost on the train. Until his parents are contacted, and he is repatriated back to his home, he will be with us."

Then he turned towards Kushal, pointed towards a stack of mattresses that were kept in a corner and said, "Choose any one of those as your mattress." Then he pointed towards one corner of the hall and said, "That will be your sleeping spot. Breakfast will be at 7, lunch at 1, and dinner at 8. All meals to be taken only in the canteen. If you are late, you will miss your meal. Only one shower a day is allowed. If you face any problems, let me know."

∞

"It's been three months since I came in here, Sudhakar Garu. Is there any news from my parents?"

"I haven't heard anything from the police as yet."

Kushal found it strange that despite it being about 4 months since he had gone away from home, his parents had made no attempt to contact him. "Have they given up on me? Have they abandoned me? Don't they want me anymore? Am I on my own now?"

He was lost in thought when he felt a hand on his shoulder. "What are you thinking so much about, Kushal?" It was Vikram, a couple of years older than him and one of his fellow inmates at the shelter. Vikram's parents had divorced when he was 7, and since neither had the means to support him, the court had ordered that he be kept at the Children's Home till such time as he turned 18. Kushal had struck up a friendship with him within the first few days of being at the shelter.

"Not thinking about anything" said Kushal

"I know what you are thinking about," said Vikram.

"Is that so? Then tell me what I'm thinking," said Kushal.

"You are thinking about why your parents haven't contacted you yet."

"That's true. How did you know?"

"Can I tell you something, Kushal?

"Sure, tell me, Vikram."

"Look, brother, if your parents haven't established contact with you even 4 months after you left home, you must now accept that they have either given up on you or, in an even worse case, they are not interested in having you back." said Vikram

"That's not possible," said Kushal. "My mother and my Ajji love me way too much to abandon me."

"All this talk of love, shuv is all bogus Kushal. Humans are selfish by nature. Finally, it all boils down to whether your parents think you are worth it or not and in both your and my case, it's quite clear that we are not deemed worth it."

Kushal didn't say a word.

"We have two options, Kushal. Either we stay in this home until we reach the age of 18, after which we will be thrown out anyway, or we escape from here and live our life on our own terms."

"What exactly do you have in mind?" asked Kushal.

"Tirupati is the largest pilgrimage centre in India, possibly even the world. 100,000 devotees visit the temple every day to pray to Lord Venkateshwara. Pilgrims visiting the temple are usually in a very charitable mood. If we just beg at the footsteps of the temple, we will collect alms of at least Rs. 200-300 every day. This will take care of our food and clothing. At night, we can sleep in the bus station. Who knows what the future holds for us? Most importantly, our destiny will be in our own hands rather than just waiting in this shelter for the road roller called fate to run over us"

Silence prevailed. "So, what do you think, Kushal?" he asked.

After a short pause, Kushal said, "I'm in."

"Good. This Sunday is when we escape from here... to our freedom," said Vikram.

"And a new life," said Kushal.

∽

Suhas's phone rang. Inspector Gaitonde was calling. "Hello, Inspector, good morning," he said.

"Good morning, Suhas," said the Inspector and then quickly continued, "I have good news and bad news for you, Suhas."

"Yes, sir, please tell me, sir," said Suhas, his heartbeat racing in anticipation of what the Inspector was going to say.

"Well, the good news is that Kushal was traced to a Children's Shelter in Tirupati."

"Tirupati? How did he get there? Thank you so much for this news, Inspector! Just so relieved to know that he is alive and well," said Suhas

"The bad news is that just when we told the Tirupati police that we were sending a policeman from here to get him back to Mumbai, we have been informed that he has fled from there along with another inmate. They are both untraceable as of now."

"Oh my God!" exclaimed Suhas. "When will our misery end?"

"Tell me, Suhas," said the Inspector. "Were you really tough on him as a father?

"No Inspector, just the normal father-son dynamic prevailed between us. I thought my wife and mother-in-law spoiled him. He was too much of a child, I wanted him to show a bit more maturity, that's all."

"Well, he has been all by himself for the past 4-5 months now. He has possibly endured some tough times during this period. It wouldn't have been easy for a 10-year-old to be all by himself with no support. Looks like the child who left Mumbai has now become an adult," said the Inspector and then disconnected.

Two Years later:

"So, what do you think, Kushal? Was escaping from the children's home a good decision or not?"

"Yes, it was," said Kushal. "It's been about 2 years now. We make just about enough money to cover our food, and sometimes, on a good day, we have a little surplus as well."

"Good," said Vikram. "I'm glad things worked out."

"But," said Kushal, "how long can we continue like this? We can't be begging for the rest of our lives. Let's try and find a job in a restaurant. We will get paid, our food will be free, and we can sleep there at night - a proper roof over our heads, instead of sleeping at bus shelters as we do now. You know how terrible it gets for us during the rains."

Vikram thought it over for a while. Then he said, "Agreed. Let's do that. For starters, let's go to all the Dhaba's that we know of. We speak to the managers and owners asking for jobs. Any job. Hopefully, some door opens for us."

For the next 3 months, they knocked on the doors of every hotel and every Dhaba in Tirupati. The owner of Happi Family Dhaba, Mr Satyanarayana Reddy, known to be a businessman with a heart, seemed interested.

"You'll say you want a job. You're so young. What can you do?" he asked.

"We can do anything, Garu. We can wash utensils, mop floors, we can help your cook in the kitchen, wait tables, home delivery... anything." They replied

"Business at the Dhaba is certainly doing well. We have more customers than we can handle with our current staff. During peak hours, a lot of customers are dissatisfied with our speed of service," he said. "I could do with some additional hands. One of you can help the cook in the kitchen and one of you can wait tables."

"Thank you, sir. Just give us a chance and we will prove to you our worth with our hard work."

"I'll pay you Rs.3000 a month. Food and shelter will be taken care of. Plus, at Diwali, I'll give you a bonus of Rs.500."

"Thank you, sir, but just a request, can you please make our salary Rs.5000? We will work very hard, sir, we promise," said Vikram.

"No. This is the best I can do. If you are not interested, you can leave."

"We will take it, sir. Please don't get angry with us," said Kushal.

"Okay, you can join from tomorrow. Our manager here will show you your tasks."

"Thank you, sir," they both said in unison.

"Oh, and there is just one thing. The police have clearly told us that we cannot hire anyone without an Aadhaar card. I hope both of you have got your Aadhaar cards."

"No sir, we don't," said Vikram.

"Oh, well then you first get your Aadhaar card done and then come here."

"Sir, can you tell us how to get the Aadhaar card done?" asked Vikram.

"There is an Aadhaar card Centre just next to the Post Office. You go there, they will take your biometrics and within a week, the card will be at your home."

"Sir, we are both orphans. We live on the street. We don't have a home; can we give your Dhaba as our residence address?"

He looked at both intently. There was a certain innocence about them that tugged at his heartstrings. "Normally I would have said no, but seeing that both of you are so young and have a desire to work hard and do something with your lives, I want to help you. So, I will say yes."

"Thank you, Garu," they both said in unison.

The next morning, they both reached the Aadhar Centre. Vikram went in first, filled in the forms, completed his biometrics, and was out in 10 minutes flat.

Next was Kushal's turn. "Place your left hand on this machine, all fingers... Good. Now your right hand, on the machine, all fingers... good."

Biometrics exist. Request denied: flashed on the technician's computer

"I can't do your biometrics; they already exist in the system," he said to Kushal.

"Already exist?" he asked. Then after a pause and some recollection, he added, "Yes, I remember now, my parents had done my Aadhar when I was in Mumbai."

"Ask them to courier the Aadhaar card to you. Or you can go to a cybercafe and download it. Do you know how to use a computer?" asked the technician

"No" said Kushal

"Do you know your Aadhaar number?"

"No"

"Well, that's it. Nothing more I can do. You can leave now and, on your way out, ask the next in the queue to come in," said the technician.

∽

On the Aadhar database, when Kushal's biometrics were being taken, there was a ping indicating a match with his earlier biometric data. In a matter of seconds, it was cross-referenced with the Mumbai database. Almost instantaneously and an alert flashed on Inspector Gaitonde's phone.

'He is still in Tirupati, trying to get his Aadhaar done,' he muttered to himself. He dialled the Aadhaar Centre from where the biometric match was found.

"Hello, this is Inspector Gaitonde from Vikhroli Police Station in Mumbai."

"Good morning, Inspector," said the technician. "How can I help you?"

"There was a 12-year-old boy who came to do his Aadhar biometrics this morning. His name is Kushal Bansode."

"Yes, sir. His fingerprints had a match, so it was a case of duplicate biometrics which were picked up by the system."

"Yes, exactly. Is he still there?"

"No sir, he left immediately."

"Has he given his contact number?"

"No sir"

"What address has he given on the application form?"

"c/o Happy Family Dhaba, Balaji Nagar, Chandragiri, Tirupati, Andhra Pradesh"

"Is there a contact number for the Dhaba?"

"Yes, sir, it's a landline, 0877 2436782."

"OK, got it. If he comes back again, you will call me immediately. My cell phone number is 9836745890."

"Yes, sir," said the technician, and they both hung up.

He then dialled the landline number in Tirupati

"Hello, is that Happy Family Dhaba?"

"Yes," said the voice at the other end.

"This is Inspector Gaitonde, Mumbai Police. I want to speak to your owner. Please get him on the line."

"Sir, I am Satyanarayana Reddy, the owner. Is there a problem?"

"There is a boy by the name of Kushal Bansode, about 12 years old, who has given his residence address as your Dhaba for Aadhar purposes."

"Yes, sir, not only him, there was another boy as well. Both approached me for jobs in my Dhaba. Such small kids just begging on the streets. I felt sorry for them and offered them jobs. Is there a problem, sir? Are they involved in some crime?"

"No," said the Inspector. "Kushal has run away from home. He is from Mumbai. It's been more than two years. We have been looking for him ever since."

"Oh! Is that so?"

"Look, they are desperate for the job and will come to meet you again, either today or tomorrow. I have spoken to the SP of Tirupati. There will be a plainclothes officer stationed at your Dhaba today itself. As soon as they come, we will nab him and detain him in the local police station."

"Understood, sir."

"It's quite a simple operation, really," said the Inspector. "I'm counting on you to make it a success."

"Sure sir. Shouldn't be a problem," said the Dhaba owner

A day later, Inspector Gaitonde received a call from the SP's office in Tirupati.

"We have got your boy, Inspector. He is with us."

"That's great! Well done!" said the Inspector. "I will take tomorrow morning's flight from Mumbai. Hope to be there by tomorrow evening. Till then, please take good care of him."

∽

Suhas was out on a delivery when his phone rang. He looked at the screen. It was Inspector Gaitonde. He immediately picked it up.

"Hello Inspector."

"Hello Suhas, Finally, I have some good news for you. We have located and detained Kushal in Tirupati. He is at the SP's office there. I am going there tomorrow to bring him back to Mumbai and hand him over to you."

"That is the best news I have heard in my life, Inspector. You can't imagine what this means to us. Thank you very much, Saheb. It's been more than two years since he went missing, but you kept trying. Even when we were down and out, you kept making us believe that one day you will find him, and now you have. You are like a God to us, Inspector Saheb. How can we repay your debt?"

"It was my duty, Suhas. I told you, I have a son of around the same age, so I knew exactly what you were going through. I'm glad it all worked out. It took us more than 2 years, but we finally found him. He will be with you by day after tomorrow."

"Can't wait, Inspector. Let me share the news with my wife straight away. You cannot imagine how happy she will be when she hears this"

∽

The Air India flight from Mumbai to Tirupati touched down at 3 pm with a 1.5-hour stopover at Hyderabad. There was a police car waiting for Inspector Gaitonde at the airport, which drove him straight to the SP office. He found Kushal seated in the visitors' room with a constable standing guard over him.

"Hello Kushal, I'm Inspector Gaitonde from Mumbai."

Kushal didn't say a word.

"I've been looking for you for 2 years, Kushal. Found you at last. Your parents were so worried about you. For a little boy like you to be all alone for more than 2 years, you are extremely brave, I must say."

Kushal didn't say a word.

"Aren't you happy to see me? I've come all the way from Mumbai to take you back, to your home, to your parents...."

Kushal fell at the Inspector's feet. "What are you doing, Kushal?" he asked.

"Saheb, I don't want to go back home."

"What? Are you insane? You don't want to go back to the comfort of your home? To your parents who love you so much?"

"No Sahib, I want to live by myself, live my life on my terms."

"You want to do what? Do you realise that you are just 12 years old? You have your whole life ahead of you. You can be back with your parents, go back to school…. live a normal life like 12-year-olds do. Living all by yourself is not easy, young man."

"I may be just 12, but I have seen more of the world than most 50-year-olds have. I've realised that in this world, you come alone and go alone. Self-interest and benefit are all that matter. All this talk about love, parents, family, relations, it's all humbug. You are the sole arbiter of your destiny and your life. I may succeed or I may fail, but it will be my life that I want to live on my terms."

The Inspector was lost in thought. "I know why you don't want to go back," he said. "It's because you hate your father, isn't it? That's why you ran away from home in the first place, isn't it?"

"No, Saheb, I don't hate my father. He was right. My mother and grandma had pampered me so much that even at the age of 10, I would behave like a 4-year-old. All he wanted for me was to grow up. Well, you can say I took his advice very seriously," he said with a wry smile and then he continued. "How is my mother? And my beloved Ajji? And my little sister Kaushalya?"

"Your Ajji passed away, Kushal. The shock was too much for her to bear. Your mother was on medication for quite a while, but is better now. Your baby sister Kaushalya, she will be three this year. Everyone misses you, Kushal, please come back with me."

Kushal turned misty eyed when he heard of his grandma's demise. Then he composed himself and said "No Saheb,

I have made up my mind. I am not going back. Tell my parents not to worry about me. I will be fine. I will visit them sometime, but after I have made something of my life."

"So, what should I tell your dad? I had promised him that I would get you along with me."

Kushal paused for a while and then said, "Tell him I ran away again!"

They both laughed

Sahab, are you carrying a copy of my Aadhaar card by any chance? I will need it to find a job.

"Yes, I am. Here you go," he said as he handed over a copy of his Aadhaar card.

"Thank you, Saheb," he said.

"Well, goodbye Kushal. Never thought I'll get to learn a totally different perspective about life from a 12-year-old. As a policeman, I come across thousands of different types of people but I have yet to come across a braver, wiser, and more mature 12-year-old. I wish you luck in whatever it is that you wish to pursue in life. God bless you, my son. I will pray for your success. Keep in touch. Do you have a cell phone?"

"No, Saheb, can't afford it."

"Let me buy you one. Consider it my parting gift."

Suhas's phone rang. It was Inspector Gaitonde.

"Hello Inspector" he said

"Hello Suhas"

"Hello Inspector, is Kushal with you? Can I say hello to him?"

"I have some terrible news for you Suhas"

"What is it Inspector? Is he ok?"

"He gave me the slip Suhas, he has escaped again!"

Regretfully Yours

Nikhil stood on the parapet of the Bandra-Worli sea link. He looked at his watch. The dial read 2:46 am. It was a moonless dark night. The Arabian Sea, calm and tranquil, lay 30 metres below - lying in wait - like a hunter awaiting its prey. He looked around nervously, one last time. "I'm jumping at the count of 3," he told himself. He closed his eyes. "1-2-" he said, but before he could say 3, he found himself being held back by a great force which he could not overcome despite countering it with all his strength. Pinned to the bridge and unable to move, he opened his eyes and found himself face to face with a tall man, muscular and well-built, his face radiating an incandescent glow. He was wearing a dazzling white suit, his head covered in a hoodie.

"Why do you want to end your life, Nikhil?" the man in the dazzling white suit asked

"Who are you?" Nikhil blurted, still in a state of shock. "And how do you know my name?"

"I'm God," said the man, nonchalantly without batting an eyelid.

"God! What kind of joke is this? Let me go, I want to end my life," Nikhil exclaimed, exhausted from resisting the force that was not allowing him to move.

"It is not a joke. I am God. Trust me, I created everything that you can and cannot see."

"Well, if you are God, then you are the one who has caused such misery in my life. And you of all people have the temerity to ask me why I want to end my life? What kind of a God are you? Let go of me!" said Nikhil

"There are 8 billion of you humans on this planet, and sometimes a few slip through the cracks. But I'm here now, so tell me what your problem is. I am sure I can help you. Try me," said the man in the dazzling white suit.

"Where do I start?" Nikhil said somewhat hesitantly. He then composed himself and carried on.

"I was the eldest child of my parents. A brother and a sister born after me, both passed away due to illness. As the only surviving child, and because they had lost two children, I was brought up at home in a very protected and sheltered environment. I was bullied at school because I was timid and lacked confidence. When I turned 18, and just about a year after I got into college, my father had a mid-life crisis and left us to live with another woman. It was a catastrophic experience for both my mum and me. Just as we were getting over this, and it looked like our problems would now be behind us, came another major setback. I had obtained admission to one of the top management colleges in the country, I met this girl - she was my batchmate in college, we fell in love and got married. Our marriage turned out to be a disaster. We realised that we were incompatible and never really got along. We didn't divorce because our daughter was born, and we didn't want her to be deprived of her parents. To get over my problems at home, I immersed myself in work. I had a horrible boss who was nothing less than a monster. I overworked myself and had burnout. I had a heart attack at 35, survived it, but need to be on a restricted diet and medication for the rest of my life."

"Wow! That's quite an eventful life you've had," said the man in the white dazzling suit.

"That's not all! Post my marriage, my mum had to live separately and all alone because my wife didn't get along with her. She died recently, all alone, no one with her in her final moments. I was away from home, travelling for work when I got the news. My dearest mum whom I loved so much, and I couldn't even say a final goodbye to her! I live with the guilt that I left her all by herself in her old age only to die alone. The guilt does not allow me to live in peace, it kills me from inside. The final nail in the coffin was my daughter Avantika, leaving us to go abroad for her higher studies. I know for sure that she will not return to India. So now I'm stuck in a loveless marriage, extremely lonely, full of guilt, with a miserable past and an uncertain future. Nothing to really look forward to. I've retired now and realised that all the money and wealth that I have earned are of no use to me. Ending my life seems to be my best option. So let go of me and let me get done with it"

There was an awkward silence for some time, after which the man in the dazzling white suit spoke, "Some of you have it tough in life, that's just the way the dice rolls. But let me tell you, there are so many of your fellow humans who have had it much worse than you but continue to fight on, in the hope that one day their life will improve. One should never give up hope; who knows, your tomorrow might be much better? Have you tried having a heart-to-heart conversation with your wife? Maybe she will understand; maybe both of you need to change and relook at things just a tad bit, and everything could fall into place. Lo and behold! Your life would be much better, and you could enjoy your life and the beauty of all my creation!"

"We have had several such conversations," said Nikhil. "It works for a little while and then we go back to square one. There is just too much distrust and incompatibility which has built up over the past 30 years. I don't see any hope of things improving. I've considered everything and I feel ending my life is the best option. So please don't stop me." He then paused for a couple of seconds and then continued his rant, "And what do you mean by things might improve? Since you claim to be God and have created each of us, don't you know what's in store for each of us? We speak about God's plan, so what's your plan for me, God?"

The man in the dazzling white suit paused for a while, and then, looking into the vast expanse of the sea, he continued, "Contrary to what you humans believe, I don't really have a plan for each one of you. Look, I've created all of this infrastructure: the sun, the planets, the stars, the earth, the rivers, oceans, mountains, flora, and fauna, even life. But once you are born in this world, I don't really have a plan for each person. There are so many of you humans, and then there are animals, birds, fish, and all things animate and inanimate. How many things can I micromanage? It's impossible, right? So, I allow nature to do its thing. Once nature gets involved, everything is random. Nothing is predictable. Some have it good, some have it bad, some have it good and then things turn bad, and for some it's vice versa. It's a rollercoaster, this life on your planet. I think one of your scientists called Charles Darwin had a term for it. He called it survival of the fittest. You need to be mentally, physically, and spiritually strong to survive life's vagaries."

"So, when we pray to you for help... all that is meaningless? Since everything is random anyway, whatever has to happen will happen, right?" Nikhil persisted with his questioning.

"Yes and No. It's not that straightforward. Life is indeed random as I said, but if anyone can connect with me on a spiritual level, then there are times when I have intervened. Connecting with me on a spiritual level is not about how much you pray to me. There are people who pray to me several times a day, but I know what they are from the inside. One needs to be a pure soul, besides fulfilling several other criteria to be able to connect with me. There are very few such people in your world. You are one of them, which is why I'm here, to try and stop you from ending your life."

"Me? Why me? I'm not even sure I believe in God or religion. I don't pray; I'm more of an agnostic."

"I just told you. It doesn't matter if you pray to me or not. If you believe in me or not. It's the purity of your value system and beliefs that matter. You are a good human being; you have the right value system. That's why I also saved you from certain death when you had that heart attack."

"What? Really? You saved me? The doctors did say on admission to the hospital that it was not clear if I would survive, but if I survived the next 72 hours, then I would make it."

"Yes. I know, and I ensured that you made it through those critical 72 hours. Like I said, there are very few pure souls like you. I would like to ensure that people like you live as long as possible. The more people like you in this world, the more the chances that the world becomes a better place and if the world becomes a better place, I can take credit for having created a successful startup."

"So that's what this is all about? We are all a part of your startup?" Nikhil looked at him incredulously

"Yes…..and like any startup founder, I would like to see my startup being successful." said the man in the dazzling white suit

Silence prevailed for the next couple of minutes as Nikhil tried to comprehend and make sense of what he had just heard. Then the man in the dazzling white suit continued.

"Tell me, what can I do to make you change your mind? How can I bring some joy and happiness into your life?" he asked.

Nikhil paused, then after a while he said, "I would like to re-live my life very differently. If you could give me the chance to go back in time and change some of the things that have made this existing life of mine so miserable, that would give me happiness and make life worth living. But you can't do that, can you?"

"Difficult but not impossible. Tell me specifically what it is that you want to change."

"My childhood. I just want to have a normal childhood like most kids do. To begin with, I want to be born into a family where my parents don't have the trauma of seeing two of their kids die. Secondly, I would like to go to a school where I won't be bullied."

"I can make that happen. However, how your life pans out this time around, that's out of my control. It could go well and you may be very happy with how things go, but on the flipside, things could go badly as well. In short, I can change your circumstances but I can't control what happens thereon. Are you willing to take that chance?"

Before Nikhil could reply, he said, "Since you blame me for all your problems and I want to make it up to you, I'll throw in a lifeline which you can use in case things don't go to your liking."

"And how will this lifeline work?" asked Nikhil.

"Here's how it will work. I'll give you a password. If you are unhappy with how your new life is going, you just have to say the password three times in your mind, and you will be instantly teleported back to where you stand right now." After a pause, he said, "Deal?"

Nikhil thought about it. Things couldn't get any worse than they already were. Besides, he had a fallback option, a lifeline, and could return to his current state if things didn't pan out as per his wish in the new avatar. He reckoned he had nothing to lose. "Deal" said Nikhil.

"OK, now close your eyes and you will awaken in your new existence as a 6-year-old. You will of course carry all your old memories, only your situation will change. Since you love your mum so much, I'll keep your mum the same but your father will be a different person. If you do have siblings, they will not die. Does that cover all the changes you wanted me to action?"

"Yes," said Nikhil.

"Close your eyes," he said and then whispered the password in Nikhil's ear. "You need to memorise it," he said. He then proceeded to place his hand over Nikhil's head and recited a mantra. When he had finished reciting the mantra, much like quantum particles that pop in and out of existence, both had vanished.

∾

"Norbert, it's time to wake up. Time to get ready for school."

Norbert slowly opened his eyes and rubbed them. He recognised his mum. "Good morning, sonny boy. How are we today?" she said and showered him with cuddles and kisses.

"Good morning, mummy," he said. Then he looked around, took in his new surroundings, and asked, "Where's daddy?"

"Daddy is sleeping, son. He came home late last night."

His mum got him ready for school. The school bus came at 8.30 am sharp. On his way out of the house, in his parents' bedroom, he saw his dad sprawled on the bed, fast asleep. In the school bus, it was all squawking and chattering with his classmates. He found school to be fun; the teachers seemed nice and friendly. A nice circle of friends with whom he played, and had a generally good time. "So far, so good," he told himself.

When he reached home, he met his father for the first time. Peter D'Costa was about 5ft 8in tall, thickset, with a shaggy beard and an unkempt moustache.

'Daddy,' he said and went towards him to hug him. Peter did not reciprocate. 'You can show some affection towards him; he is only a child,' said his mother.

"He is not my child," said Peter menacingly. "I was away on work for a week and when I came back, you told me that you are pregnant. God knows whose child it is."

"How can you say that, Peter? I fell in love with you and we got married. It's been 7 years now. Do you have no conscience to accuse me of infidelity? You are a third-class person with a third-class mentality. My parents were right when they said that Peter will make your life miserable. I'm paying the price for not listening to them," his mum wailed as her tears flowed.

"I'll show you who is third-class," said Peter. Norbert heard the noise of a slap and saw his mum fall. Norbert rushed to his mum. Little droplets of blood came out of her mouth. "Mummy," he cried.

"It's okay, son, don't cry" she said.

Peter got dressed and left the house. "I won't be home for dinner," he barked on his way out.

"You are too young to understand this," she whispered to Norbert. "Once you grow up, you will understand. Truth is, I fell in love with your daddy and am paying the price for my decision to marry him much against my parents' wishes. I thought he would change after marriage but I was so wrong."

Month after month, he saw the same episodes being repeated. He realised his father was an alcoholic and would beat his mum regularly. His mum silently bore it because she had nowhere to go. She had married him against her parents' wishes; their door to her was shut. To make matters worse, she wasn't financially independent.

One night, when things between his parents got bad, he decided that he had had enough. There was no way he wanted to spend the next 13-15 years of his life in this atmosphere. That night, when his mummy had tucked him into bed and he had said goodnight to her, he closed his eyes, said the password three times, and in an instant found himself transported back and standing on the parapet of the Bandra-Worli Sealink. The man in the dazzling white suit was standing next to him.

"What happened?" the man asked. "I changed everything as per how you wanted it. But you still came back?"

"My father was a good-for-nothing alcoholic who beat my mum. I couldn't bear to see her suffer. How could I live in that house?"

"I told you, I can change your situation, but I can't change what happens thereafter."

There was a quiet pause as they both reflected on the events that had transpired. The man in the dazzling white suit asked, "So, how can I help you now?"

"Can you make me go to the same MBA college that I graduated from, but this time, I don't want to be friends with the girl I fell in love with. I would like to befriend and marry someone else."

Sure. But again, please note, as it happened the previous time, I cannot guarantee how things will work out for you. It might... It might not..."

"I'll take that chance. If it works, good, if not, I'll be back here, right?" Nikhil asked.

"You got it"

This time, he knew the protocol. He closed his eyes, the man in the dazzling suit placed his hand on Nikhil's head, said the mantra, and 2 minutes later, just like the previous time, both had vanished.

Insert the idea or change of setting break design here

The Indian Institute of Management Ahmedabad, was the premier Management Institute in the country and attracted the best of student and faculty talent. The Marketing Strategy Class was in session. Professor Raghuram Bhatt was speaking to the students: "Today we will learn about Michael Porter and what he says in his book Competitive Strategy for Competitive Advantage."

From his seat, he could see Janki. "Gee, I'm not going anywhere near her," he thought to himself. He was lost in his thoughts when he heard the professor mention his name.

"Nikhil, can you summarise for the class the highlights of Michael Porter's Marketing Strategy?"The entire class turned its gaze on Nikhil, waiting to see what would happen next.

"Michael Porter speaks about three things a business should follow to be competitive in a business environment. They are Cost Leadership, Differentiation, and Focus. You can either have a strategic advantage by being the lowest-cost producer, or have a differentiated product/service offering, or focus on a very narrow niche where others do not want to enter because it's not attractive enough."

"Good. Thank you very much, Nikhil," said the professor. "I thought you were dreaming, but you were paying attention after all."

After class, Supriya walked up to him. "Hi, Nikhil," she said.

"Hi Supriya"

"Well, that was good, the way you answered Prof Bhat in class. We all thought Prof Bhat had put you on the spot there.

"Nearly was, but you can call it divine intervention that saved me," said Nikhil. They both cracked up.

"Where are you from, Supriya, and which college did you study at?" he asked.

"St. Stephens Delhi, majored in Economics Hons. And you?" she asked

"IIT Powai, Mechanical Engineering"

"Engineer, so you must be good at Maths. Can I ask you some of my queries in Linear Programming? It's alien to us non-engineers."

"Sure, he said. I'm free this evening. Let's meet in the college library, and I can try to help."

"Cool," she said. "See you in the library at 6."

Over the next couple of months, they began meeting quite regularly, often over coffee, studies, movies, and chess. Two years later, they graduated. She was placed with Deloitte in Delhi and he with Hindustan Unilever in Mumbai. Friendship had turned into love. The entire batch knew by then that they were a couple.

He had introduced her to his parents, and she had also introduced him to her parents. The plan was that they would get engaged in about a year and get married the following year.

About 6 months into her job, Supriya broke the news to Nikhil.

"Deloitte is offering me a transfer to New York as head of their Hedge Funds vertical. I really want to take it. You can join me there. We can stay in NY, the Big Apple!"

"That's great news! Delighted for you!" he said. "But how can I join you there? I have my own job with Unilever and career here in India. If you think it's a good career move and want to take it up, we will have to be in a long-distance relationship. Will that be good for us? Please think it over."

"I really want to take it up," she said. "It was my dream to work in NY."

'OK,' he said. 'If you feel that strongly about it, then you go. We can have a long-distance relationship and hopefully at some point in the future, either you will come back or I will join you in NY.'

"Oh! Thanks, Nikhil for understanding and supporting me! You're the best! Love you!" Supriya was ecstatic.

A month later, Supriya had left for New York to take up her assignment.

Their relationship would now be long-distance. Technology did offer various options for them to keep in touch, with video calls being the closest alternative to being present in person. The first week without each other's physical presence, was the hardest. Gradually they reconciled to the fact that they would just have to manage this relationship this way. They just couldn't wait for Sunday evenings, when they would connect on video call.

And so, things continued for the next 8 months. Video calls on Sunday, WhatsApp calls and texts during the week, things were in cruise control, or so Nikhil thought. So, one day just out of the blue, when Nikhil received a WhatsApp message from Supriya which said "We need to talk. Urgent and important," he didn't know that a bolt of lightning was on its way to hit him.

"I'm sorry to tell you this, Nikhil, but I really think we should move on," she said after initial pleasantries were exchanged.

"What? Supriya, is this your idea of a joke? I don't think you should say this even as a joke," he had said.

"No, Nikhil, I'm serious. This long-distance relationship isn't really working."

"I know," he had said. "I did tell you when you got your transfer that a long-distance relationship would be very tough on both of us. But you insisted…"

"To be honest with you, I've developed feelings for a guy here from the office. We both like each other. We started out as office colleagues, who then became friends and before I knew it, I realised that I had fallen in love with him and knew that he was the one I want to spend the rest of my life with," she said. Nikhil tried his best to convince her to give their relationship some time; he even said that he could fly down to NY to meet up with her to sort things out, but Supriya had made up her mind. As far as she was concerned, the relationship was over.

Nikhil was devastated. Grief-stricken and heartbroken from losing the love of his life, he decided to bail out. That night, he had a few drinks to drown his sorrows. When he hit the bed, he said the password three times and found himself back again in the same place on the Bandra-Worli sea link, face to face with the man in the dazzling white suit.

"Now what?" said the man in the dazzling white suit. "I hope there was no mistake on my side? I did everything that you asked me to."

"Yes, you did," said Nikhil, acknowledging that there was nothing more that could have been done to help him. "Things didn't work out for me this time either, but thanks to you, I learnt a lot of lessons about life which I believe will keep me in good stead."

Is that so?" asked the man. "And what is it that you have learnt?"

"I've learnt three lessons, if that's what I may call them," said Nikhil. "And I will remember them for the rest of my life." He then continued

"Lesson 1: Life is like a game of cards. Each one of us at birth is dealt a set of cards. The cards that you get are not in your control; how you play the game of life with the cards that you have, that's in your control. Complaining and regretting about the cards you have will not help. You need to find a way to make do and succeed with the cards that you have."

"Sounds interesting. What's the second thing that you've learnt?" asked the man.

"Sometimes, despite your best efforts, you don't succeed. Running away from reality doesn't help. It's best to face reality head-on. If things are tough, make plans to mitigate your tough circumstances; if things are good, maximize your potential. Bide your time till things turn for you. Good times or bad times, both don't last forever."

"OK, noted. And the third?" asked the man

"Since two or more people are involved in a relationship, Communication is the key. When we fall in love, or when we get married, we tend to overlook our partner's needs, desires, ambitions, in short what makes the relationship tick. Recognising that and ensuring that channels of communication are kept open always is very important. Even a small wound in a relationship should be treated immediately, if allowed to fester, it can turn into gangrene and then amputation is the only solution."

"You're absolutely right," said the man in the dazzling white suit. "Even I, as God, couldn't have summed up life's lessons as well as you have." After a pause, he continued.

"So, no suicide anymore, right?"

"Nope. From today, I will look at life from a whole new perspective," said Nikhil.

"That's so good to hear, Nikhil. I'm glad that I could be of help. I will not be around each time you have a problem, so put what you have learnt to good use going forward..."

"Yup, I will," said Nikhil, wiser from the whole experience.

"Tell me, what would you like from me as a parting gift?"

"Anything that's okay with you, God."

"I would like to show you my creation and all its wonders. Would you like a quick tour of the Universe?"

"The entire Universe?"

"Well, some parts of it. The entire Universe will take too long. I can show you the solar system of which your planet Earth is a part."

"Sure, God, would love to,"

"Good. Just hold onto me tightly and close your eyes."

Nikhil did as he was told.

Now, open them

He found himself whizzing through the solar system faster than the speed of light. The moon, resplendent in its silvery hue, just flashed by in a couple of seconds. Then Venus shining brightly, then Mercury, then the sun.

Wow! The sun! exclaimed Nikhil. It's massive and it's hot! Never thought I'd see it from this close. How did you think of this, God? Thermonuclear Fusion to power the sun....

"I needed a source of energy to keep the solar system going. That's the physicist in me finding a solution to the energy problem."

They continued onwards, "That's Mars! It's so red!" exclaimed Nikhil.

"God... Why did you make Mars red?"

"That's the artist in me. What's a solar system without a bit of colour?"

Then onto the gas giants they went. There was the massive planet Jupiter and then Saturn with its rings.

"Why did you give Saturn rings?"

"Oh Saturn! I wanted to explore my creative side. All the planets were spherical and looked identical in shape, so I said let's have one with some rings attached. Just to break the clutter."

Uranus, Neptune, and Pluto flashed by in the blink of an eye

"Why is Pluto so small compared to all the other planets?"

"I wanted to have some symmetry. The sun as the largest celestial body at one end and Pluto as the smallest at the other. But your scientists now say that Pluto is not a planet anymore, so that didn't quite work out, did it? Sometimes even God's best-laid plans don't work out," he said with a wink and mischievous smile.

"Oh wow! That was too good! Almost magical!" said Nikhil as he found himself back at the parapet of the BWSL. "I will never ever forget this day, God. Thanks for everything and, more importantly, thanks for saving my life."

"Well, it was nice meeting you, Nikhil. I wish you all the very best. May you be at peace with yourself in this journey called life."

"Thanks God," said Nikhil,

"Goodbye Nikhil," said the man in the dazzling white suit, and then he vanished.

"Goodbye God," said Nikhil.

∽

The incessant beeping of the alarm clock woke Nikhil up. He rubbed his eyes, which then settled on the wall clock opposite him. It was 7 am, Sunday morning. He recollected vividly everything he saw in his dream. It took him quite a while to get out of bed. Finally, he got up, stretched himself and got out of bed. He brushed his teeth, and then started to boil some water to make his cup of tea. Normally he would make just a cup for himself but this time he made two cups. He then went to the living room where his wife was reading the newspaper. They had been living and sleeping separately for more than a decade now. Communication between them had reduced to hello and goodbye - sometimes even that did not happen.

"Good morning," he said to his startled wife, who couldn't believe what she had heard. At first, she thought he was on a phone call, but when she looked up, she saw that it was Nikhil speaking to her.

"Good morning," she said, still in some shock.

"I've made some tea for you. Would you like some tea?" he asked.

"What! Yeah, sure, that'll be nice," she said.

"Here you go," he said and gave her the cup.

She was still a bit dazed when she took the cup that he had offered her. It had been almost three decades since their relationship had been in a state of disrepair, so she was unprepared for what was unfolding.

"Is there something you want to tell me?" she asked. She wasn't sure what Nikhil was up to.

'I've figured out,' he said, 'that we can spend the rest of our lives hating each other and carrying grudges. In short, we could live a miserable existence, or we can say, "Look, our marriage was probably a mistake, but that doesn't mean that we must live as enemies forever. We can be civil to each other, and still make the most out of this situation that we find ourselves in, within whatever limitations we have."

She looked at him in shock and bewilderment.

Nikhil continued, "I agree that there has been a lot of bad blood between us over the past 30 years. A lot of mistrust and misunderstanding has scarred our relationship. Going forward, we possibly cannot be very friendly with each other. But look at it from the practical side. We are both in our sixties now. Do we want to divorce at this age? Will that be a solution? If we live into our eighties, just the fact that we live under the same roof will be of great solace and comfort. God forbidding, if one of us falls and breaks a leg or has a heart attack, one of us can call the ambulance, right? Avantika will be 10,000 km away. An old age home could be an option, but that comes with its own set of problems." Then after a pause, he added, "What do you think?"

"I've been saying this for years," she said, "but you just would not listen. Thank God, you have now realised it. Better late than never, I guess," she said, still not fully convinced that what she was hearing was for real.

"Yeah," he said. "Thank God. But I'm not done yet. There is one more thing I need to do." He then picked up his phone and made a phone call to his daughter in the US.

"Hello Avantika,"

"Hey dad," Avantika replied.

"Hope I'm not disturbing you on a Saturday evening,"

"No dad, it's fine. We didn't have any classes today. I'm just chilling in my room with my friends."

"Look, Avantika, I wanted to tell you that when you decided to go to Boston in the US for your Master's programme, I was deeply upset, even angry with you. I mean, you were the only child and everything that we had, right? So, when you decided to move so far away, I thought it was heartless of you. That you were a selfish person who didn't care about her ageing parents.

"I'm sorry, dad, but..."

"No, no, you don't need to be," he interrupted her. "I just needed to tell you this and get it out of my system. I understand that as a parent, I needed to give you a good upbringing, a good education, make you independent and then allow you to take charge of your own life. This is part of nature's law. Like a bird one day, leaves the safety of its nest and flies away to make its own future.

"Dad..."

"So, I just wanted to tell you that I fully understand and support your decision, and will stand by you and support you, no matter what."

"Oh, I'm so happy and relieved to hear this, dad. While you never told me directly, I always knew that you were not happy with my decision and the guilt of leaving both of you alone was eating me up from inside. I am so happy to hear this. Thank God for this change of heart, dad," she said and then continued, "But I'm curious to know what has brought about this change? Have you started following Sri Sri Ravishankar or something?" Avantika said and then had a hearty laugh.

Nikhil laughed "Let's just say it was God's plan," he said.

"God's plan?" she asked in complete disbelief. "But you don't believe in God, right? You're agnostic."

"That's another story for another day. I'll tell you in more detail when we meet. It's an interesting story…."

Divinity

Panaji, Goa:

'You are tuned in to Goa FM 93.1. The next song is a country classic, first recorded by American Country singer Marilyn Sellars in 1974. Enjoy…' The singer's mellifluous voice filled the car… *I'm only human, I'm just a woman, help me believe in what I could be and all that I am. Show me the stairway that I have to climb, Lord for my sake, teach me to take one day at a time. One day at a time Sweet Jesus, it's all I'm asking of you…*

"Ah, my God!" screamed Veronica. She was on her way back home from the office. "Sorry, madam," said her driver, apologising profusely, "Didn't see that speed breaker." He parked the car and went over to the passenger seat at the rear. He helped her to get up and get seated again. 30 painful minutes later, they reached her home. Next morning, when she woke up, she found herself unable to get out of bed and decided to seek medical attention.

"Belfer's Clinic," said the voice on the phone.

"Hi, I'm Veronica, and I would like to fix an appointment with the Orthopedic Surgeon, Dr. Kamat."

"Thank you for calling," said the receptionist. "Dr. Kamat is available today at 7pm. I'll book you an appointment. What may I write down is the complaint?" she asked.

"I have a severe backache," Veronica answered.

"Seems to be a slight misalignment of the C6 vertebra in your spine," said Dr Kamat after he had finished examining her "We need to get an MRI done and also run a few blood tests to see what could be the problem for you to have so much pain."

Four days later, she was back at Dr Kamat's clinic

"The MRI looks okay," he said, "just some small bruising, but your blood test results seem to be all over the place. The WBC count is way up; some of the other counts are also out of whack. Do you have any other health-related issues?"

"I have not been eating too well of late, doctor, and my friends and colleagues at work tell me that I appear to have lost some weight over the past 3-4 months. Of late, I do feel tired and exhausted, but I haven't checked my weight as such," Veronica replied.

"For your back pain, all you need is a supporting belt and a lot of rest. I'll also prescribe you some medication and some physiotherapy exercises; you should be fine within 15 days. However, your blood test results need to be checked out. You need to see a physician to check you thoroughly. I think you should see Dr. Borges. I'll refer you to him. Fix up an appointment and see him," Dr. Kamat advised.

A week later she was back at the Belfer Clinic, this time Dr. Borges was examining her:

"I've seen your blood and MRI reports. Can we start from the beginning? What is ailing you? What symptoms are you having?" he asked.

"I fell in the car, after which there is some pain in my back, although the severity has reduced now. I also have no appetite and struggle to eat. There is this dull pain in my abdomen which persists all the time. I've lost weight and feel tired all the time. Initially, I thought it was the stress of my job but it's been quite a while now…." her voice trailed off.

"Where do you work?" Dr. Borges asked.

"I work at Goa 365," she replied.

"Ah Yes, I know that channel," Dr. Borges said. "We watch it occasionally."

"I'm the VP of Content Creation there," she said.

"That's nice. What's your family like? Are you married?" he asked.

"I live with my parents," she said. "I'm not married."

"Boyfriend?" he asked

"No," she said quite emphatically.

Motions? Periods? All okay? When was your last period? He asked.

"My motions have been alternating between loose motions and constipation, and as for my periods, they also alternate between being very heavy flow and very scant. My last period was about 15 days ago."

"OK," said Dr. Borges, "Let's do two things."

"One, let's do an endoscopy followed by a colonoscopy to check out your digestive tract. There could be an infection there from what you describe, and two, I would recommend you see your gynaecologist and get yourself examined."

A week later, she had a clean bill of health from the endoscopy and the gynaecologist. The colonoscopy, however, had encountered a problem. "We couldn't get the probe through your colon," said the technician. "There appears to be a blockage; we need to check whether it's faecal matter or what is causing the blockage. A CT scan of your intestine needs to be done."

The following Monday morning, when Veronica went to the office, her boss and the owner of the channel, Mr. Nayak, asked her to come into his room.

"Hi Veronica, how are things?" he asked.

She looked at him and shrugged. "OK, kind of. Why do you ask, sir?"

"I've been noticing that you are taking a lot of leave these days, for medical reasons of course, but just thought I'd check. You do look quite run down."

"I'm just sick and tired of all these tests. I just hope everything is okay with me," she said.

"Relax - I'm sure nothing is wrong with you. All you need is a break. The story you broke on the sand mafia in North Goa has maybe left you overly stressed. The more doctors you visit, the more they will torture you with their never-ending tests." Then after a pause, he added, "Let me give you some free advice - As far as possible, always keep away from two coats - The black coat, which is the lawyer, and the white coat, which is the doctor."

"I agree, sir. Both are too painful to handle," said Veronica - both had a hearty laugh.

∽

A week later, the CT Intestine scan results were in. Dr. Prabhudesai had her reports on his table. He looked grim as he called her to his chamber.

"Well Veronica, I'm afraid the news is not too good."

"What is it, doctor?" she asked, her heart beating rapidly in anticipation of the bad news.

"The CT scan clearly shows a tumour in your colon. It may or may not be cancerous. We don't know yet. We need to run a biopsy and a few more tests to check if it's cancerous or not. If it is cancerous, it could be a Kruckenberg" tumour. Extremely rare, this one. This tumour typically manifests itself in the gastrointestinal tract and then spreads into the ovary."

"Good God! Of all the things, do I have cancer? Is it curable, doctor? Will I survive? If not, how much time do I have?"

Veronica's head was exploding with shock at what she had just been told.

"Whoa, whoa, please hold your horses," said the doctor. Firstly, we do not know if it's cancerous. Secondly, and even if it is, modern cancer therapy has progressed quite a lot. Having cancer does not mean a death sentence anymore. Look at Manisha Koirala, Sonali Bendre, and a whole lot of others who have beaten cancer and are doing quite well. There are treatments available. You need to see a cancer specialist in Mumbai straight away without wasting any more time.

A week later, the biopsy results came. It confirmed that the tumour was cancerous and had spread to her ovaries as well. The doctors in Goa had advised her to consult the cancer specialists in either Tata or Nanavati, two of Mumbai's hospitals that specialised in cancer treatment.

Veronica was shattered but wise enough not to spread the news. Only her parents, her sister, and her best friend Nancy knew. In the office, other than her boss Mr Nayak, no one knew. Mr Nayak was, of course, highly supportive. He had told her that she could take as much leave as she wanted for her treatment without worrying about her salary or job security.

Anyone who interacted with her after her diagnosis could now see a different Veronica. Withdrawn, brooding, inward-looking, lost in thought, contemplative. Mentally and physically, it had taken a big toll on her. Nancy her childhood friend, would meet her quite regularly and try to cheer her up.

"Worrying won't help you, Veronica. You need to motivate yourself and stay positive to fight this disease," Nancy tried to keep up her spirits.

"I will fight it to the last ounce of energy I have," said Veronica, "But, I'm just wondering, just how cruel life can be. I've never harmed a soul in my life. Been respectful to all whom I've interacted with, worked diligently at my job, always helped those who were in need. What did I do wrong? Of all the people in this big wide world, why have I been chosen for this? Why me?"

"There is no easy answer," said Nancy. "Sometimes life throws us a curveball, we need to figure out a way to handle it and reclaim control of our life."

"Do you think I will die?" "I don't want to die," tears flowed down Veronica's eyes and her voice trailed off.

"About death, no one knows when and how it will come. But it will come for sure. For you, me and every living being on this planet. So why bother about something that's not in your control? As the saying goes, Control the Controllables," said Nancy. Then she paused for a while and said, "I've heard of a father in Karwar called Father Stephen. From what I'm told, he gets some kind of revelations about the person's future when he puts his hand over them and prays. Some say he has some kind of hotline with God! Try him out, but you need to book an appointment. You leave for Mumbai in about a week to see the surgeon, so call up his ashram tomorrow and book an appointment. He is booked for months in advance, but tell them about your diagnosis and surgery, and they will help you break the queue."

Veronica didn't say a word, just stared blankly.

"Hello! Madam, you're lost in thought. I know you are not a terribly religious person, but this is more spiritual than religious. I think it's worth a try. You have nothing to lose anyway. I can help in getting you an appointment..."

"I'll go," Veronica interjected.

Karwar, Karnataka:

"Thanks for coming with me, Rach," Veronica said as she hugged her sister Rachel who was at the wheel for the 2-hour drive from Panaji to Karwar.

"Oh, come on, sis, it's the least I can do for my elder sister," said Rachel.

"You have your own family, two small daughters to look after, so I can understand it must have been difficult to do at such short notice," said Veronica.

"Damien has taken the day off to be at home. He is being the good husband!" she said, and they both had a good laugh. Throughout the drive, Rachel tried to keep the mood light but engaging Veronica with various funny anecdotes which had happened during their growing up years. By 9 am, they were at Father Stephen's Ashram gate.

Rachel parked the car and they headed towards a signboard that read Reception.

"We have an appointment with Father Stephen," said Rachel.

The nun at the reception desk went through a thick register and found their names. "Please wait here, Father will see you soon" she said.

They looked around. From all the certificates and trophies that adorned the reception area, they could figure that Father Stephen's Ashram in Karwar looked after the unwanted, homeless, and uncared-for people.

After a wait of about an hour, a nun ushered Veronica into the Father's room.

"Veronica, welcome my child," he said. "I'm Father Stephen, what brings you here?"

"Father, I have been diagnosed with cancer of the colon. I'm going to Mumbai next week for surgery. I am very frightened and worried. I don't know if I will survive. I have come with great hope to you. Can you please pray for me and tell me what's in store for me?"

"Of course, my child, I'll pray for you," said the Father. "Don't worry and don't lose heart. God has his own plan for each one of us. Sometimes he tests us with adversity to see how resilient we are. In adversity, is our faith still strong enough? Do we keep faith or do we jump ship?"

"I'm just 40; I don't want to die. There is so much more I would like to do and achieve in life…."

"Don't worry my child, let me pray for you," said the Father. He then put his hands on Veronica's head, and closed his eyes, and went into a meditative state, praying silently. This continued for a while. After some time, he broke out of his trance and opened his eyes.

Seeing that the father was now out of his trance, Veronica was quick to ask "What do you think, Father?"

"Tell me a bit more about yourself," he said. "Tell me something about your parents, your family, your education, and work. I want to know more about you…"

Veronica answered all his questions, and then after a bit of pause and reflection, he said the three magical words that she was looking for: "From what I see, you won't die. Not immediately anyway. What intrigues me is that when I prayed over you, I found Divinity in you. It was as if there was some power within you and it was communicating with me. I was told 'She will suffer a lot, and that will make her a stronger person but she will survive this and go on to do a lot of good in this world." Then, after a pause, he asked, "Tell me, are you very religiously inclined? Have you had any visions of God in your dreams, etc.?"

"No, Father" said Veronica, "Other than attending Sunday mass and going for my confession, I'm not very religious."

"Well, I wish you all the best," Father Stephen said, "But remember, there is divinity within you. It's only when you realise it, that your life will change and you will make a difference to the world."

Mumbai, Maharaashtra:

A short flight from Goa to Mumbai and a quick taxi ride later, Veronica found herself at the Nanavati Hospital in Vile Parle, Mumbai. Established in 1951, the hospital had undertaken several rounds of modernisation to keep up with the times. This included a spanking new cancer wing where Veronica found herself seated just outside the chamber of Dr. Kulkarni, the main Surgeon, and head of Gastroenterology.

In an hour's time, he called her in. He was flanked by a team of 4 other doctors. "We have seen and studied all your reports," he said. "We can't waste any more time. It's a Kruckenberg tumour, confirmed by both the CT scan and the biopsy. It's quite advanced, possibly in the 4th stage. We need to operate immediately. I'm fixing the day after tomorrow for the surgery. Get admitted to the hospital today itself. You need to be fasting from tomorrow morning onwards in preparation for the surgery."

The surgery itself was a complicated affair; the team of four doctors needed 7 hours to perform it. After what seemed like a forever wait, Dr. Kulkarni finally came out of the OT and spoke to Rachel, "The surgery is done, it went off quite well. We have successfully removed the entire cancerous part of the colon, which was about a metre in length."

"So, doctor, what are her chances now, post-surgery?" Rachel asked.

"To be extremely honest with you, the prognosis for these types of cancers is not too good. She will need to undergo chemotherapy for the rest of her life. And even after that, I would say that 3 years is the best-case scenario for her. While we have removed the affected part of her intestine, in almost all such cases, the cancer recurs in 2-3 years. And when it recurs, it's even more potent than before, invariably metastasising and spreading to a lot more organs." said Dr. Kulkarni

"So, what do you think we should do now doctor?" a stunned Rachel asked

"I'm sorry to say this but once she recovers from the surgery, she should be encouraged to live her life and do all the things that she wishes to do. Let her enjoy her life to the fullest. She won't be around for very long, honestly speaking," said Dr. Kulkarni after which he left the room

All Rachel could do was sob her eyes out at the unfairness of it all. To know that her sister would be with them for just a few more years was an unbearable thought, but she needed to stay strong - for her parents and her sister's sake.

∽

"It's nothing short of a miracle," said Dr. Mudassir, who was now in charge of her treatment post the surgery. "The latest PET scan again confirms that your cancer is in remission.

A 4th stage cancer in full remission after 2 years of surgery… Well, to be honest with you, we had not expected an outcome as good as this. You should consider yourself extremely lucky, young lady."

"Thanks for all your help and support, doctor," said Veronica. "Without your constant help and support, I'm sure I wouldn't have made it this far. Just knowing that I will live for some more time means so much to me, doctor."

"We as doctors apply the medical science that we have learnt to the best of our abilities," he said. "But if you ask any of us, we will be the first to acknowledge that sometimes medical science cannot explain everything, and your case is one of them. All I can say is someone up there likes you," he said with a wink.

"That's nice of you to say," she said, "but tell me, doctor, when can I stop the chemotherapy? It's got all these horrible side effects. Will I be able to lead a completely normal life like other people do? Or is that too much to expect?"

"As I've told you, Veronica, stopping chemotherapy entails a huge risk. The side effects of chemotherapy, yes, they are horrible but are still manageable with medication. However, if we stop the chemo and your cancer recurs, not even God can then save you. The final decision is yours of course, but I think you need to know this before you take any decision."

After a pause, he added, "There could be a way out though. It's a long shot, but maybe you would want to give it a try."

"I'll try anything, doctor. All I want is to lead a normal life and do the normal things that other people do."

Dr. Mudassir continued, "The Sloan Kettering Hospital in New York has come up with a new breakthrough in this regard," he said. "They do what is called DNA sequencing of your blood and in doing so, they can predict with a good amount of accuracy if your cancer will come back or not on stopping the chemo. Would you like to look at this option?"

"Of course, doctor," Veronica nodded her head vigorously.

"Dr Richard Dreyfuss and his team at the Sloan Kettering Hospital have pioneered work in this. You can Google him. Send his office an email and arrange a Zoom call with them. They will guide you on the way forward."

New York and Rome:

The Air India flight from Mumbai to New York was full of both businesspeople and tourists. Veronica had gotten her US and Schengen visas quite quickly. She had spoken to Dr. Dreyfuss on Zoom (along with Dr. Mudassir) and explained her case. Having understood the background of her case, Dr. Dreyfuss was happy to meet up with her and fixed an appointment at the Sloan Kettering Hospital in New York. On the way back, she planned to visit Rome - specifically the St. Peter's Basilica to pay her obeisance, to say thank you to Jesus for having given her a new lease of life from what seemed to be a hopeless position.

She booked herself into the 31ˢᵗ Street Broadway Hotel in Midtown Manhattan. The hospital was just a 10-minute walk from there. She reached the hospital for her appointment well before time. At the appointed hour, she was ushered into the office of Dr Dreyfuss.

"Good morning, Veronica. How are we doing today?" the doctor asked, a big smile on his face.

"I'm fine, doctor."

"All the way from India. That's a really long flight, isn't it? When did you reach New York?"

"Two days ago, doctor."

Got over the jet lag? Are we all good to go?

"Yes doctor"

"Well, we have gone through your entire case history, studied all your reports and done some detailed analysis. We now need to run a few tests which will further enhance the accuracy of our predictions. The end objective of our entire procedure is to have a better understanding of where your cancer stands right now and the probability of it continuing to be in remission if the chemotherapy is stopped."

"Yes, doctor, that's my understanding as well," she said.

We conduct several highly advanced tests, including DNA sequencing and gene splicing. We will take samples of your blood, tissue, and hair and run them through various tests. The entire testing process should last about 2 days, and your results should be available 2 days after that.

"OK, doctor. I understand," she said.

"Let's get started right away," he said.

The tests were done in 2 days just like the doctor had said. The staff at SK were simply superb as they wheeled her through the various departments and tests. Then followed a 2-day agonising wait in her hotel. On day 5, she was back in the hospital and in the doctor's chamber.

"Good morning, Veronica, how are you doing today?" the doctor was his normal cheerful self.

"Quite Nervous, doctor."

"There is no need to be nervous, Veronica. I have some very good news for you."

"Really, doctor," she said, a faint smile appeared on her lips.

"Yes, all your tests show that the probability of your cancer coming back is very slim. It's not zero, but it's very slim. Almost negligible you could say. This is indeed a miracle considering your cancer was in the 4th stage," Dr. Dreyfuss told her. "Go and enjoy your second life. All the best!"

Veronica's joy knew no bounds. She called up Dr. Mudassir and her sister Rachel, followed by her friend Nancy and her boss at the office, and gave everyone the good news. After close to 3 years of being at the receiving end, she was finally free to live her life as a normal person. She was booked to be in New York for the next couple of days, and she decided to live it up. She explored all the touristy places in New York, shopped in Broadway, ate her favourite pizzas and gelatos, and generally had a ball. When it was time to leave, she packed her bags and left for JFK airport in New York en route to Rome.

She boarded the Alitalia flight from New York to Rome and after refreshments were served, she drifted off to sleep.

Unknown to her, right from the time she boarded the flight, Bishop Daniele, whose seat was on the aisle opposite to her, was observing her closely. Upon landing at the airport, he followed her to be within earshot of the cab driver whom she had hired. Upon reaching his residence, he called his trusted aide, Giovanni. "There is an Indian lady by the name of Veronica Coutinho who has checked into Hotel Torino," he said in Italian. "I want you to follow her tomorrow and report to me on where she goes."

The next morning, Veronica booked an Uber from her hotel to St. Peter's Basilica located in the heart of the Vatican. The Basilica itself was an imposing structure - the most beautiful church in the world. Intricate sculptures, the papal crypts in the Vatican grottoes, and paintings by Michelangelo adorned the walls. She climbed to the top of the cupola, all of 320 steps leading to fantastic views from where the entire city of Rome could be seen.

Having done the touristy part of seeing the Basilica, Veronica then went to the main church to say a prayer of thanks. She knelt and was deep in prayer. Unknown to her, Giovanni was observing her from a distance and kept the bishop posted on what she was doing. When he told the bishop that she was deep in prayer, the bishop passed on some instructions to him in Italian.

Having finished her prayer, Veronica was surprised to see two guards of the Chapel standing next to her. "Excuse me, madam," one of the guards said in their broken, halting English heavily laced with an Italian accent. "There was some problem with your entry papers into Italy yesterday at the airport. There is an officer from Immigration wanting to speak to you. If you could please join us, this way, please."

"I'm sure there has been some mistake," said Veronica. "Are you sure it's me you are looking for?"

"Yes," said Giovanni. "Veronica Coutinho from India. Came to Rome from New York last night by Alitalia flight no. AZ 764. It is you, right? There is no mistake from us."

"Yes," she said. "It's me alright. What is the problem? I have a valid Schengen visa. It was checked by the Immigration Officer at the airport last night."

"I don't know about that Madame; an Immigration officer is waiting for you at the Sistine Chapel wanting to ask you a few questions. so, if you will follow us, please," said Giovanni

"If you insist, and I have no choice" said Veronica, and followed him. 'Mistaken identity for sure,' she muttered to herself.

The Sistine Chapel was in the same compound, just next to the Basilica - a back door from the Basilica led straight to it. The Chapel itself was the Pope's official residence. Originally known as the Capela Magna, the Chapel's fame lies mainly in the frescoes that decorate its interior, most particularly the Chapel ceiling and the Last Judgement both painted by Michelangelo

Giovanni led her through the Chapel and onto the courtyard, from where there were some steps that led to another building. She climbed about two flights of stairs and found herself in a room where Bishop Daniele Salera was waiting for her.

"Good morning, Madame," the bishop said.

"Good morning, Father. Seems like a case of mistaken identity, Father. I'm not sure why I've been asked to see the Immigration Officer," she said.

"I asked them to get you here," said the bishop.

"You did? Why, Father? What do you want from me?" she asked

"I'll tell you why, my dear child," he said. "First, tell me something about yourself. Where are you from in India? What was your childhood like, and what brings you here?"

"Well, as you know, Father, my name is Veronica Coutinho, and I'm from Goa in India," Veronica began. Over the next hour or so, she told him everything about herself, her family, her childhood and upbringing, her education, job, diagnosis with cancer, how she survived and beat back the disease, her US visit to Sloan Kettering, and how she was in Rome to visit the Basilica to say thanks to the Lord Jesus for having saved her.

The bishop heard her patiently and after a bit of a long pause, said to her, "Well, my child, there is something I would like to share with you which is very, very confidential, and you should not share it with anyone else. Please promise me that."

"Sure, Father, you have my word," she was still not clear on where this entire thing was leading to.

"I belong to an organisation called the I Descendenti. In Italian, it means The Descendants. We are a very small sect of only about 500 people, but we are spread across the world in all the various continents and countries. We believe that Jesus survived the crucifixion due to his spiritual powers, escaped to India, got married and raised a family. We have historical and scientific evidence to prove all of this, but due to various political and religious reasons, we can't come out in the open. So, everything we do, is done in a super confidential way and in the shadows. We are part of the church, but they do not know about our existence."

"What?" Was all a shocked Veronica could muster. And then after a while she asked, "So, where do I fit into all this?"

"The I Descendenti aim to trace those who we believe are the descendants of Christ. We believe such people exist in various parts of the world. Much like some Buddhists are trained to recognise the reincarnations of the Dalai Lama, the members of I Descendenti are trained to notice and read signs in those who we believe are the descendants of Christ," the bishop said.

"Wait, Wait, Father… So, you think that I am…?" Veronica's voice trailed off.

"Yes, there is a certain spiritual vibe that the descendants exude, and you can say we are trained to latch onto it. Much like a transmitter and receiver. Only if the frequencies of both matches, do you have a connection. You exhibit all the traits that we look for. For one, they are put into extreme situations just like Jesus himself was put into, like when he was crucified. They are given no hope of survival, sometimes even given up for dead. It's been 2000 years, encompassing about 100 odd generations, and so the descendants have spread far and wide across the world. There was this brave girl, for example," the bishop went on. "She was shot in the head by fundamentalist forces in her country for advocating women's rights to education. She survived it, and today she does a lot of work for women's rights and helps a lot of women in distress. Similarly, there are others, to give you another example, there was this lady from Romania who had a very difficult childhood with lots of hardship and suffering. Growing up, she devoted her entire life to caring and healing the sick and needy in India. There are several such examples that I could give you. We will take up the whole day if I start to narrate all of them."

Stunned silence prevailed in the room as a speechless Veronica just stared blankly at the bishop.

"There is also a gentleman whom I believe you have met," said the bishop.

"I have met him? Can't seem to remember meeting any such person. Who would that be, father?" Veronica asked and looked at him quizzically.

"Father Stephen of Karwar," said the bishop. "You met him at his ashram, right? He called me and told me about you. Our people in India have been keeping tabs on you since then. We wanted to meet you in India itself, but when you made plans to go to the Sloan Kettering Hospital in New York and then return to India via Rome, we decided to wait and meet up with you here in Rome."

"Really Father? You knew of me when I was in India itself? And you knew about my travel plans and everything?"

"Yes, we did," said the father and then continued, "Look, Veronica, your diagnosis was of colon cancer in the 4th stage. Very few people survive that. The surgery you went through, the 100 odd chemotherapy sessions that you have gone through. These are not things that mere mortals can survive. You are special, Veronica, you had better believe that."

"I still can't believe this, Father. I am not even very religious," she said.

"Being very religious and devout does not necessarily characterise the Descendents. There are other signs in you as well that we noticed. You have always been a crusader for justice. Remember the sand mafia story you investigated and published on your TV channel, despite the threat to your life? This is another typical trait of the Descendents. After hearing your story, and with our experience of seeing the signs and identifying the Descendents, I am convinced."

"I'm a Descendent" she asked incredulously. "Well, If you say so, Father... What exactly does it mean?"

"Well, what it means is that your survival from cancer is not a fluke. It is because you have been kept alive to fulfil a higher purpose. You must identify that purpose and devote your entire life to fulfilling it. You have great powers which at this moment are unknown to you, but you will get acquainted with them one day. If you use these powers properly, you can bring about great change in this world. It is now your sacred duty to use this power and bring about change for the better in this world."

"If what you say is true, father, I certainly will try to," she said.

"You certainly are my child," said the bishop,

Veronica was spellbound and had nothing to say, just trying to comprehend the full import of what she had just heard. Then the Bishop spoke up.

"That is all I have to say, Veronica. Goodbye and good luck. We will keep our eyes and ears open to see what change you bring about."

"Goodbye, Father," was all that Veronica could muster.

The Air India flight from Rome to Mumbai was rather uneventful. Throughout the flight, and even when she drifted off to some very intermittent bouts of sleep, Veronica was preoccupied with thoughts of her meeting with the bishop. The entire meeting and conversation kept playing in her mind on a loop. Somewhere on that flight, all the pieces of the jigsaw that were swirling around in her head seemed to fit, and things became clear to her. She had made up her mind on what she wanted to do henceforth and going forward.

Karwar (Two years later):

Father Stephen woke up at his usual 5.30 am, said his prayers, and by 7 am was ready for breakfast

At the breakfast table, he would normally read the newspaper. On page 5, there was an article that caught his attention.

Under the headline, BCGP launches data portal, was the following article.

To improve the understanding of the genetic variations of cancer in India, The Bharat Cancer Genome Project (BCGP) has launched a data portal which aims to be a repository for India-specific cancer Genomics. This portal aims to benefit researchers in providing tailored cancer treatments for patients.

"Historically, cancer treatments in India have been based on Western datasets. However, cancers in Indian patients can differ significantly at the molecular level. This is a portal where the genetic signatures of Indian cancer patients would be stored and would be of immense use for researchers in curating bespoke treatments for Indian cancer patients," said Ms. Veronica Coutinho, the Chairman of BCGP.

He then mulled over the article for a bit before picking up his phone to speed dial a number in Rome.

"Hello Bishop" he said when the person at the other end picked up the phone.

"Looks like Veronica has started her mission in this world,"

"Yes Father Steven. Her true purpose in this world is to help the scientists find a cure for cancer. We should provide her with all the support that she needs in accomplishing this," said the bishop before hanging up.

Tom & Jerry of the Universe

Jan-Feb 2021: Satan's Abode - somewhere in the Universe:

In his hot, smoke-filled, dimly lit meeting room, aptly called The Hell Hole, Satan was addressing his team of daredevils. "I am happy to announce a resounding victory over God, and the destruction of planet Earth… finally we have won!" he said to loud and raucous cheers.

"That's fantastic, Master! How did you finally beat God?" one of the daredevils piped up.

"It's quite funny how things work on planet Earth. They have divided their planet into many countries, and each country is ruled by a leader. Most of these leaders are low on intellect but very high on ego and narcissism. There is also a huge ongoing tussle between the number two and number one country for global supremacy. Seeing an opportunity, I brainwashed the leader of the number two country.

'You can be the number 1 in the world by destroying other countries' I whispered in his ear.

He fell for it and got his scientists into developing and unleashing a virus so strong, so contagious, so incurable, and so fatal that the poor humans on planet Earth just didn't know what hit them! Half the population is dead, and the other half is just waiting to die. It's been about a year since the virus was first unleashed, but they have found no cure for it. Another six more months of the virus doing its thing, and there will be no human left on the planet. Game Over!" said Satan.

"Victory, Victory," said the daredevils in chorus.

A daredevil mustered up all the courage at his disposal and gingerly asked, "Master, what about God? Didn't he try to save the planet like he usually does?"

"God is either dead, or he has accepted defeat and given up," Satan said to a cacophony of noise.

Raising a glass of human blood as a victory toast, he shouted "Hip, Hip,"

"Hooray!" screamed the daredevils in unison.

He then turned towards Lucifer, his trusted lieutenant. "So, Lucifer, what's happening these days on planet Earth? Show us what's going on there. I hear Earth has become a very happening place these days…"

It's Showtime! Lucifer exulted as he clicked a few buttons on a machine with ***Live Relay from Earth*** written on it in big bold letters. A giant LED screen lit up as did his face.

Lucifer added his own commentary to the video feed: "As you can see, there are dead bodies piled up everywhere. They have run out of space to even bury or cremate their dead. Hospitals have run out of both doctors and beds. Those alive are walking around with masks, much like zombies. The deadly and contagious virus has not discriminated between the young and the old. It announces itself with an ordinary cough and cold, and ends up suffocating and choking them to death. There appears to be no escape for them!"

"Saaytan, Saaytan," the devils broke into a rhythmic chant. Much like the cricket-crazy Indian crowds would do when their favorite cricketer, Sachin Tendulkar, was batting.

Tears of joy welled in Satan's eyes. "You guys have no idea how tough it's been. How hard I've tried to achieve my goal, which was to destroy planet Earth, and how God has ruined it every single time," he said. Going down memory lane, he continued...

"I first tried 4.5 billion years ago. Planet Earth had just been born. I nudged Theia, another similarly sized planet, to collide with it. The resultant collision caused it to disintegrate. It lost 30% of its mass. The resulting debris from the collision was flung 200 thousand km away into space. That should have spelled the end for planet Earth, but out of nowhere, God appeared on the scene and transformed the debris into Earth's Moon. Its gravitational pull stabilized Earth's spin and it emerged stronger than before."

"We shall overcome," the daredevils sang in unison.

Satan continued, "A billion years later, I tried again. I made it rain nonstop for 2 million years. The entire planet drowned in water. Just when I thought the planet would meet its end in a watery grave, lo and behold! God made the sun shine with a much higher intensity. The heat evaporated all the excess water. The water that remained on the surface of the Earth, formed the oceans from which the first life forms on Earth began."

"We will never give up," the daredevils sang in unison.

"My third attempt was 66 million years ago, when dinosaurs roamed the planet. I commanded Chicxulub, a 15-kilometre-wide asteroid travelling at a speed of 100 km/second, into striking it. The impact created a crater that was 93 miles across and 12 miles deep. The resultant shockwave and heatwave ejected vast quantities of debris and soot. The sun was blocked out. Photosynthesis stopped. With the death of all plant life, there was no food for the dinosaurs to eat nor any air to breathe. They all died out in a matter of years."

"That should have been the end, right?" Lucifer interjected. "How on Earth did Earth survive?"

Satan was now visibly angry and agitated. "Everything that lived on the surface of the Earth was destroyed. However, a species called mammals, which lived in burrows under the Earth, survived and later evolved into apes and then humans. And thus, intelligent life was born."

"Patience is the key," the daredevils sang in unison.

"I tried a fourth time as well. 85 years ago, in 1939 to be precise. I created a monster called Hitler and convinced him that he belonged to a superior Aryan race. That his sole mission in life was to rule the world and destroy all other humans, especially the Jews. I gave him access to the best military technology prevalent at the time."

"Then what happened Master?" Lucifer was curious.

"Hitler killed 6 million people - gassed them to death in specially made gas chambers. It was called the Holocaust. He began World War 2, invaded Europe on his way to conquering the world. But just when he was about to conquer Russia, the winter that year turned extreme. It froze and jammed all his military equipment. Hitler was defeated, and the war ended. In the post-war era, there was peace and stability. People on the planet prospered."

A deathly silence enveloped the room.

Satan looked visibly downbeat and lost after recounting all his failed attempts. Realizing that the mood in the room had turned sullen, Lucifer intervened. "The long wait is over now, Master. Very soon you will be crowned the 'Emperor of the Universe.' We need to celebrate this great victory. Let's booze, dance, sing. It's party time!"

While all the daredevils left the meeting room to get ready for the party, Satan continued to sit on his high chair and think aloud, 'I wonder where God is and what he is up to. Is he really dead? Or will he once again come out of nowhere and yet again spoil my party?'

Jan-Feb 2021: God's Abode - somewhere in the Universe:

I'm a Barbie girl in a Barbie world, made of plastic, it's fantastic... God's Personal Assistant and Gatekeeper to heaven, Archangel Gabriel's phone rang. His ringtone was a matter of much discussion amongst the inmates of heaven. "How and where did you get that ringtone, Archangel?" one of the angels had asked him.

"Got it from a teenager's phone," he had replied. "She died clutching her cell phone. Both came to heaven together. She got a call from her friend on Earth, and that's when I first heard it and loved it! So, I quickly downloaded her ringtone onto my phone."

He peered through his horn-rimmed glasses into his specially curated and encrypted phone. It was Michelangelo - the angel in charge of Earth who was calling.

"Hello Mikey, what's up?" and before Michael could respond, he continued, "Whatever it is, Mikey, you had better make it quick. I'm swamped with work these days - 24x7 nonstop. There seems to be an unending queue of humans on Earth who have died and are waiting to be interviewed. As you know, my job is to personally interview each one of them, and only those that pass the interview make it to heaven. The rest rot in hell!"

"Archangel, I'm sorry to disturb you, but I believe there is a matter that needs God's urgent attention."

"Go on," said the Archangel.

"Reports are coming in of some very disturbing events on Earth. I've tried my best to resolve it, but it looks like it's beyond me. Where can I find God? I haven't seen him around for about a year now."

"He is away on a top-secret mission. He has asked to be contacted only in case of an emergency."

"It's an emergency alright. Something is badly amiss on that planet."

"I'll see what I can do," said Archangel Gabriel and hung up. There were a whole lot of questions that were bubbling within him. Where is God? What's the emergency on Earth that Michelangelo was referring to? Did it have any connection with his increased interview workload?

After some thought, he entered a highly secure and access-controlled area called heaven's Communication Room. Inside, there was a giant machine with *"Telepathic Communicator"* written on it. He switched on the machine.

A voice from the machine said, "If you want to communicate with God, press 1."

Moving on to the next menu, it said, "If it's urgent, press 1."

Jan-Feb 2021: Mt. Olympus Mons - Planet Mars:

God was wearing a pensive look. It was his life's mission to seed two planets namely Earth and Mars with life. He did create life-supporting conditions on both, but while he had succeeded with Earth, his Mars plan had failed. After showing initial promise, the magnetic field, atmosphere, and water he had created on Mars vanished. All that was left was a desolate and barren landscape incapable of supporting life.

His chosen species, the humans on planet Earth, had turned greedy and brought it to the edge of a precipice. They had engineered climate change, wars, disease, and exhibited a shocking lack of concern for the environment. He estimated that in the next five hundred years or so, planet Earth would not be habitable for humans. He was angry with them for what they had done to his beloved creation. But, like any parent would, he believed it was his responsibility to bail out his children when they were faced with a difficult situation.

'I need to create another home for the humans of planet Earth. Mars needs to be made habitable for humans,' he told himself.

He surveyed the Martian landscape from the top of Mars's highest mountain - Mt. Olympus Mons. At 72,000 feet, it was 2.5 times higher than Earth's highest mountain, Mt. Everest. He could see the polar ice caps which once contained water but were now permanently frozen. If he could melt the polar ice caps, the water it would release would start flowing back into the dried-up river beds. This would, in turn, kickstart the Martian ecosystem into supporting life. As a first step, he had gotten the American space agency NASA to send a mission comprising a Rover and a Quadcopter to explore and gather data about the planet. But, without his help and intervention, chances of NASA succeeding were remote.

He was lost deep in thought when the telecommunicator on his wrist began to beep.

From the Martian night sky, he could see Earth. He wondered what the problem could be, but from the tone and tenor of Gabriel's call, he knew the matter was urgent. He pressed a button called Teleport on the gadget attached to his wrist.

Jan-Feb 2021: Cambridge, United Kingdom:

What he saw on Earth horrified him. There was a deadly virus on the loose causing death and destruction on a scale he had never seen before. 'Satan is at it again!' he told himself. 'This time he has unleashed a deadly virus. Since it's a medical problem, I need to find a medical solution.'

He pressed a few buttons on the telecommunicator. Michelangelo appeared on the screen. "Mikey, which is the most renowned pharmaceutical company on Earth, well known for its R&D in vaccines?" he asked.

Michelangelo did a quick Google search and then replied, "Master, that would be AstraZeneca, headquartered in Cambridge, UK."

In an instant, he teleported himself to the AstraZeneca HQ. Chief scientist Dr. Susan Gilbert was having a discussion with her team of scientists in the meeting room. He effortlessly took control of her brain and spoke through her voice.

"Team members - we are amid an unprecedented crisis. We need to develop very quickly a vaccine that can fight the deadly COVID virus. I have a plan that I think will work."

Our lab technicians reveal that there is only one protein on the surface of the COVID virus. We could use the chimpanzee adenovirus vector from the MERS vaccine, which has been tested and found to be safe. We know it can provoke immune responses. Now all we need to do is to copy and paste the genetic code for the spike protein onto our harmless chimp adenovirus to create the vaccine. With the right teamwork, we can do it within 3 months. What do you guys think?"

"Yes, ma'am. We can do it!" the scientists said in unison.

"Come on, guys! Let's get cracking!" she said.

By May 2021, the vaccine was developed, tested, and ready for mass manufacture. For a world with a population of 8 billion people and two shots per person, 16 billion doses had to be manufactured in the shortest possible time.

"Mikey, which country has the infrastructure to make 16 billion shots of the COVID vaccine in the shortest possible time at the lowest possible cost?"

"Master, only one country comes to mind, India,"

"Which company in India?"

"Serum Institute in Pune,"

June-July 2021: Pune, India:

The head of the Serum Institute of India, a very respectable and well-known figure in the field of vaccine development and manufacture, was addressing a press conference.

"We have signed an agreement with AstraZeneca to make 16 billion doses of the Covishield Vaccine. To do this, we will have to set up a new factory next to our current one. This will help increase our production capacity to 2 billion shots per month. The government of India has already given us the land, and all the necessary permissions are in place."

I can assure you that in 8 months, we can deliver the 16 billion shots that the world urgently needs. We can thus rid the world forever of the menace of this deadly virus.

Christmas Eve, December 24th, 2021: Goa, India:

"One more beer, please," an innocuous-looking tourist seated in a corner table said to the bartender of Titos Bar and Pub in Candolim. The tourist was clad in a white t-shirt and Bermuda shorts, wearing a sombrero hat and Oakley sunglasses. Almost all the countries had vaccinated their population, the virus was in retreat, and people were now slowly getting back to their normal way of life. The restaurant was crowded, festooned with Christmas and New Year decorations. There were revelers everywhere, dancing, drinking, all having a good time. There was a DJ who was playing party and hip-hop music.

The tourist looked around contentedly. Seeing people who were happy, and alive and enjoying themselves gave him the most satisfaction. He looked around and his eyes settled upon a large-screen television. CNN was broadcasting the news.

"NASA today suffered a major setback in its bid to explore and gather data on Mars. Both the Perseverance Rover along with the Ingenuity quadcopter suffered mishaps yesterday. The latest satellite imagery showed that Ingenuity was beyond repair as it had lost one of its four blades. One of the cameras on the Martian Rover Perseverance was also not functioning after a dust storm engulfed the planet. Stay tuned for more updates…."

The tourist shrugged his shoulders, 'He never gives up, does he?' he said to himself. He then gulped down his beer and called out to the bartender.

"Can I have the bill, please?" he said.

"You're leaving so soon, sir? You've just had two beers. Not partying through the night on Christmas?" The bartender tried to cajole the tourist into not leaving early. Customers partying longer meant larger bills, which invariably meant larger tips.

"Would love to, but something urgent has come up," said the tourist.

"Oh, sir, how sad! It's tough to have work to attend to on Christmas when everyone else is partying. I'm sure it must be urgent for you to leave the party. Anyways, I'll get you the bill, sir," said the bartender and left the table.

When he came back, he found that the tourist had disappeared. Just plain vanished out of sight. He looked around but couldn't find him. He found it strange because he hadn't seen him leave the table.

His heart missed a beat. If a guest left without paying, the bill amount would get deducted from his salary. He looked at the table. The tourist had left behind cash on the table, which more than covered the bill amount. He had also left behind a Post it. He picked up the cash and read what the tourist had scribbled on the post it. 'Merry Christmas to you and your family, Pedro. Thanks for your hospitality. All the very best!'

He turned towards his colleague and fellow bartender, Cajetan. "How did that guest know my name?"

Cajetan was busy serving customers. "God knows," he said and walked away